# The
# Quilters
# Club:
## Next Generation

## A Quilters Club Mystery

ABSOLUTELY AMAZING BOOKS

Habent Sua Fata Libelli

# ABSOLUTELY AMAZING BOOKS

Manhanset House
Shelter Island Hts., New York 11965-0342

bricktower@aol.com • absolutelyamazingebooks.com

The Absolutely Amazing eBooks and Books colophons are trademarks of J. T. Colby & Company, Inc.

**Library of Congress Cataloging-in-Publication Data**
Rockwell, Marjory Sorrell.
Next Generation #21.
p. cm.
1. FICTION / Mystery & Detective / Amateur Sleuth.
2. FICTION / Mystery & Detective / General.
3. CRAFTS & HOBBIES/ Quilts & Quilting.
Fiction, I. Title.
ISBN: 978-1-955036-89-4, Trade Paper

August 2025

# The
# Quilters
# Club:
## Next Generation

A Quilters Club Mystery

(Book 21)

A Young Quiltmakers Mystery
(Book 1)

Quilter Club Mysteries

# Quilters Club Mysteries

## By Marjory Sorrell Rockwell

**Available from**
**AbsolutelyAmazingEbooks.com**

"A Quilters Club book
without the Quilters Club—what gives?"


—Maryjane Elizabeth Jones,
author of *The Phantom Cooks* series

# Table of Contents

# INTRODUCTION

**B**ook 20 was supposed to be the last Quilters Club mystery. So, what do we call this one – a continuation of the characters in a different (and future) time period?

Some literary scholars might describe this as a Stand-Alone Sequel. Or a Future Sequel. Or a ... never mind.

Call it what you like – but this mystery takes place several years after the last book in the series, yet involves some of the characters from the previous Quilters Club stories – namely, Aggie, N'yen, and Sissy. Hopefully, you remember them, Maddy Madison's grandchildren and their friend. For years, they were junior members of that cotillion of amateur sleuths posing as a quilting bee.

So, you might ask, if this book isn't an official Quilters Club mystery, why is "Quilters Club" part of the title?

Well, mainly so fans of the Quilters Club series will know that this is a new story involving some of their old friends from those prior books.

That's why it's called The Quilters Club: Next Generation. Another charming mystery from the pen of Marjory Sorrell Rockwell.

If you liked her previous stories about four middle-aged female amateur sleuths – "that marvelous quartet of Miss Marples," they've been called – then you will likely enjoy this tale of three or four younger versions, characters you have already met, but never witnessed solving crimes on their very own as grownups.

Maybe you should think of this as the opposite of a prequel. Think of it as a postscript, or a post-sequel – a book that takes place after all those stories you've previously read.

Hats off to Marjory Sorrell Rockwell for picking up where the Quilters Club mysteries left off – offering herewith what might be the first of the Young Quiltmakers Mysteries.

—Hollis George
Editor and Anthologist

# CHAPTER ONE

### Aggie's First Case

The Quilters Club was defunct. That is, its members – Maddy Madison, Cookie Bentley, Lizzie Ridenour, and Bootsie Purdue – had retired from the sleuthing game.

As many of you know, the Quilters Club was a small Midwestern quilting bee (four members, count 'em), amateur detectives who had developed something of a reputation for solving crimes: murders, missing persons, lost treasures, even lost puppies. Now, in their late sixties, it was time for the girls to pack it in, call it a day.

Sure, Maddy had given her word to the mayor – her son-in-law Mark Tidemore – to disband the group and leave the crime-solving to the Caruthers Corners police department. The new Police Chief (former Chief of Detectives Harry Teague) was quite competent. Even Maddy acknowledged that. And she could be picky.

The previous Chief, Jim Purdue, had finally make good on his threat to retire. He and his wife Bootsie had moved to Florida, choosing a retirement village with more sunshine days per year than their hometown in northeastern Indiana saw in an entire decade.

Bootsie's departure had been another reason for the Quilters Club breaking up. She was part of the glue that held the group together.

Nevertheless, the gals still reconvened ever Tuesday afternoon (as was their habit), but now by Zoom. Teleconferencing was almost like being there.

As life would have it, the four friends were drifting in different directions. Settling into their Golden Years. Each with a different agenda.

Maddy Madison turned her attention to baking watermelon cookies and cakes. And using her large trust fund for philanthropic projects that benefited the good folks of Caruthers Corners. Her husband Beauregard Hollingsworth Madison IV (Beau, for short) had stepped off the Town Council and now spent most of his days fishing on the Wabash with Lizzie's husband, Edgar Ridenour. Edgar had retired as president of the Caruthers Corners Savings & Loan many years earlier. These days Beau and Edgar were in leisurely pursuit of a legendary largemouth bass known as The Monster.

Lizzie Ridenour continued to oversee the Hoople Heritage Quilting Museum, but had given up her position as the state's quilting champion, a title she'd held for over a decade. Her fingers weren't quite as nimble as they used to be – a touch of rheumatism.

Cookie Bentley had left the town's Historical Society to manage her vast real estate holdings, her responsibility since the passing of hubby Ben. A heart attack. He was the second husband she had buried. First spouse Bob Brown had left her with debts; Ben had left her a very wealthy lady, the largest landholder in the county.

With her freakish eidetic memory, Cookie had turned out to be an excellent businesswoman. In just a few years she had doubled the estate's net worth. But, at the same time, she cut her landholdings in half by donating thousands of acres of rich farmland to the local watermelon growers cooperative.

Caruthers Corners likes to promote itself as "The Watermelon Capitol of the Midwest." It was almost true, that being the main product of this small farming community in the northeast corner of Indiana. The fertile ground stretching along the Wabash River was perfect for growing plump, juicy melons.

Agnes Millicent Tidemore – Aggie to her friends – had just graduated from Yale Law School and set up a small one-woman practice in her hometown. It didn't hurt that her dad was the town's popular mayor; and her grandfather Beau Madison was a descendant of one of the Town Founders. Business referrals were much appreciated when starting a law firm from scratch. Things were kinda slow, so she spent a lot of time helping her Grammy bake watermelon cookies.

These days her best-est friend Sissy – Cecelia LaToya Madison (née Jackson) – was the town's librarian, having taken over that position when Dorothy Stargazer retired to take care of her elderly parents. Sissy had a degree in Library Science from Indiana State University, a good school that had allowed her to attend classes online. That provided time for Sissy to get married to her longtime fiancé, Aggie's adopted cousin N'yen Madison.

Having completed his Doctor's degree in Astrophysics through an advanced placement program at Northwestern University, the young Vietnamese genius had returned to Caruthers Corners where he could pursue a work-from-home career as a senior editor for *Scientific American*. Working offsite, nobody was off put by his barely-voting-age youth. Or his superior brain power, a trait that was intimidating to most folks.

As N'yen liked to say, his editorial assignment was to write about "anything above your head" – a double entendre for coverage of astronomical advancements (and anything to do with space), as well as any other matters the average layman could not easily understand.

N'yen was *that* smart.

~ ~ ~

It was on a recent Monday that Aggie met her pal Sissy for coffee at the library. There was a Starbuck's kiosk in the far corner of the reading room, more a self-serve coffee machine than a café, but the 16 oz. grande caffé latte was the same blend that you'd find at the franchise stores with that green mermaid logo.

The library occupied the middle wing of the Perricock Museum of Science and History, that castle-like edifice overlooking the town from one of the area's twin hillocks. The Hoople Retirement Center was perched atop the other hillock, looking like two warring castles separated by a moat-like chasm.

Sissy's assistant – Tessie Humphrey, she was Errol and Janey Baumgartner's daughter – took over the front desk while she took a break with her lawyer friend. Tessie was twice Sissy's age, but had great respect for her boss's bibliothèque acumen. The younger woman could recite the entire Dewey Decimal System at the drop of a bookmark. And she could put her hands on practically any volume in the place without consulting the card catalogue – although these days the card catalogue was computerized.

"How's business?" asked Sissy as she settled onto an uncomfortable wooden chair across the table from Aggie.

Aggie shrugged. "Slow," she confessed. "No wills to draw up. No property to transfer. No miscreants to defend. Not even a client with a parking ticket to dispute."

"Hmm, seems like Caruthers Corners used to have a lot more crimes to solve. No wonder the Quilters Club disbanded."

Aggie nodded. "Harry Teague runs a tighter ship than Uncle Jim did. I think criminals have better pickings over in Burpyville."

"Well, that *is* the county seat," Sissy pointed out. "More criminals, more crimes, a bigger police department, the court system headquartered there, plenty of bail bondsmen."

"... and more lawyers."

"True. Here, you don't have much competition. It's down to you and Horace Hutchinson. He opened up shop about two years ago. All the others have faded away."

"Died or retired. Except my dad. He still belongs to the Bar."

"But he's the town's mayor. Doesn't practice anymore."

"But he could if he wanted to."

"Face it, Aggie. You may have to wait a few more years before he joins you in a law practice."

"Tidemore & Tidemore – that's my dream."

"Your dad's a very popular mayor. He'll keep getting re-elected 'til the cows come home. That office has no term limit. You're gonna be a one-man – or woman – practice for quite a while longer."

Aggie rolled her eyes, the blue irises flashing in the fluorescent lighting. "There's barely enough business for one lawyer. Lucky I've got a trust fund or I couldn't pay my rent this month."

"You don't pay rent. You bought the old Yager mansion, cash on the barrelhead."

"It was just an expression. But who would've thought I'd turn out to be a starving lawyer?"

"Sounds like a contradiction of terms."

"Starving is starving."

Sissy smiled, her white teeth a contrast to her dark skin. "Don't think of it as starving, girlfriend. Think of it as dieting."

"I still have my girlish figure. No need to diet."

"Braggart," said Sissy. She had gotten a little plump after settling down to married life.

"Look on the bright side," smiled Aggie. "Business may be slow, but that gives me time to have coffee with you here at the library."

Sissy shook her head, her straightened brown hair swaying with the motion. "How does Horace Hutchinson keep going? Business can't be good for him either."

Aggie sipped at her hot coffee, blowing on it to keep from burning her lips. "Horace got here ahead of me, snared the town's account, the watermelon co-op business, and the retirement home. Everything else is nickels-and-dimes lawyering."

"Your dad's the mayor. Why can't he give you the town's account?"

"Nepotism. He doesn't believe in it."

"That's too bad. With the annual Watermelon Fest, Shakespeare in the Park, and the Crazy Carnival, that would be enough business to keep you afloat."

"I've got Aunt Cookie's real estate account, but ever since she gave half her land to the watermelon cooperative, she hasn't had many transactions. Doesn't want to buy more, or divest anything else."

"How about the EZ Seat Chair Factory? That's the town's largest employer."

"Old N.L. Purdue has used a law firm over in Burpyville for thirty years. He's a man of habit, not about to make a change. Besides, N.L. doesn't like the Madisons. He sees us as being allied with his wayward brother, Bobby Ray."

"Well, you are. Too bad those too-rich-for-their-own-good brothers don't get along."

"Wish I could get Bobby Ray's account. He's always buying and selling companies. That would keep me busy."

"Bobby Ray would drive you crazy. He's like a Peter Pan still living in Neverland."

"More like a minor league Elon Musk with a ten-minute attention span."

"That's a fact."

"Who else then?"

"How about the Dollar General?"

Aggie shrugged. "It uses a corporate lawyer."

"The DQ?"

"Same."

"Guess that would apply to MacDonald's and Pizza Hut too?"

"You got it."

"How about –?"

Just then Aggie's iPhone rang.

"Oops, sorry," she said. "I forgot to turn the ringer off." A sign outside the library's entrance sternly stated:

QUIET PLEASE!
PHONES MUST BE
TURNED OFF
INSIDE LIBRARY.

"Don't worry about it. You're the only person here this afternoon." Sissy glanced at her watch. "Hmm, 2:15. That will change soon as school lets out. A swarm of locusts will descend upon us."

The phone continued to ring.

"Sure it's okay? It's my Dad calling."

"Hey, I'm the librarian. I make the rules. Go ahead and take it."

"Hello?"

Sissy could hear the insect-buzz of someone talking into her friend's ear, but couldn't make out the words.

Aggie said, "Yes, yes, okay. Really? Of course, I will. You know I need the business. Okay, thanks. Bye, Daddy."

"What was that about?" Sissy asked when her blonde friend put down her phone.

"Daddy says ol' Birdie Longstreet just shot someone. Says she will need a good defense lawyer. And that she's asking for me."

# CHAPTER TWO

## Birdie

**B**eatrice Camellia Longstreet was what some folks called pixilated. Most neighbors simply referred to her as batty. Nearing 90, a medical doctor might have diagnosed her with dementia or Lewy Body or Alzheimer's – but truth was, she'd been this way most of her life.

Birdie (as she was known) lived a life of perpetual confusion. Messages became tangled. Her hearing was faulty. Her perception was off kilter. She mistook school children for *Wizard of Oz* Munchkins. Stray dogs for timber wolves. Bearded Edgar Ridenour for a werewolf. She once mistook Sissy's grandfather Buck Jackson for former President Barrack Obama, the only similarity being their skin color.

The Caruthers Corners police were used to Birdie's constant complaints: reports of prowlers (Bigfoot, she claimed), intruders (turned out to be a FedEx delivery), zombies (she lived next door to the Yost & Yost Funeral Home), space aliens (little Jimmy Jinks trick-or-treating in his Halloween costume), and an escaped circus lion (Maisie Walters' prowling tomcat, Alexander the Great).

So, it was with a grain (no, make that a pound) of salt the police dispatchers took Birdie's 911 calls. When the old lady phoned in today screaming that she was being murdered, no one got overly excited … till Deputy Tommy Truehart made the customary "wellness check" and discovered a dead man lying in the entryway of Birdie's stately Victorian on North Main Street.

~ ~ ~

Not being used to many dead bodies, Deputy Truehart was somewhat discombobulated. Chief Harry Teague took over while Tommy went back to the police station to lie down on a cot in one of the two jail cells and regain his equilibrium. Fortunately, both cells were unoccupied at the moment – although Birdie Longstreet might be setting up housekeeping in one before the day was over. No question that the old lady had shot someone.

Myrtle Dobbler, who along with her lookalike sister Elvina, managed the police dispatcher's post, brought Tommy a cup of water from the cooler. "Take a deep breath," she advised him. "You'll be all right in ten or twenty minutes. Dead bodies ain't no big deal."

"Oh, have you ever seen one shot in the head?"

"Seen every kind you can imagine – shot, stabbed, strangled, burned to a crisp, mangled in a car wreck, one even put through a wood chipper."

"Really? Where was that?"

"Me an' my sister used to work as cosmetologists for Yost & Yost before we joined the police department."

"I didn't know that."

"Somebody gotta pretty up them corpses so their loved ones don't have nightmares."

Tommy Truehart gulped down his water. "I'd rather stick to parking tickets and computer work. Don't think I've got the makings of a homicide cop."

"Fortunately, we don't have too many murders 'round these parts."

"One's too many," he groaned, plopping back onto the lumpy cot.

Myrtle put on her round-cheeked Octavia Spencer smile. "Best leave the murder investigating to Chief Teague. He got lots of practice at that when he worked for the Burpyville PD. They have more crime over there than we do. Shoot 'em ups and armed robberies and gangland killings. He's seen lotsa dead bodies."

"He can have 'em."

"Who was it that Birdie shot?"

"Fritz Berber."

"The mailman?"

"Yep, he was wearing his official uniform. That's how I recognized him. His face was all bloody, shot between the eyes. That old gal may have palsy but she can shoot straight as Wild Bill Hickock."

"Oh my. I didn't know Birdie had a gun, much less knew how to shoot one."

"She said it had belonged to her late husband."

"Gordon Lochinvar Longstreet? He's been deceased for 75 years, killed in the Korean War. He was shot down by them Commies in the Battle of Incheon when General MacArthur landed with the 1st Calvary."

"Guess that explains the gun she used, a US Model 1911A1 pistol. That .45 left a big hole in Fritz's forehead. Nearly half an inch wide. And the back of his head was all but gone."

"Not as messy as a shotgun. Elvina and me had to fix up ol' Hector Schaeffer, Fat Karl's grandfather. He committed suicide with a 12-guage. Let me tell you, that was worser than a spilled pot of spaghetti sauce."

Tommy looked up from his cot. "As I recall, that was a closed casket funeral."

"There's only so much you can do with clay putty and pancake makeup," Myrtle sighed. "Death ain't pretty."

~ ~ ~

The paramedics had taken Fritz Berber away by the time Aggie Tidemore arrived at Birdie's. It was a short trip for ol' Fritz, in that Yost & Yost Funeral Home was located just next door. Doc Medford, who lived only one house over, had walked across the yard to pronounce Fritz officially dead. In his early 70s, Doc served as coroner for the county in his spare time.

"Is Birdie still here?" Aggie asked Deputy Gus Bentley, newest recruit to the police department. He was Aunt Cookie's adopted son, the six toes on each foot attesting to his one-gene-short-of-a-freak-show heritage. Otherwise, he seemed normal.

"Yes, she's inside with Chief Teague," the deputy nodded toward the door. "Why do you wanna know?"

"I'm Birdie's lawyer. She asked for me."

"Oh, okay. Guess it's alright for you to go inside in that case. Just step around the yellow crime scene tape."

"Thanks, Gus."

"You bet, Cousin Aggie."

That made her wince, but she realized that was being prejudiced. He was a Cuckoo-for-Coco-Puffs Crackleton, but so was she if one were being honest. Family trees don't lie.

The Crackleton clan lived just north of town at Crackleton Crossing. Known for their inbreeding and criminal tendencies, they were no prize in the genetic pool. People said they were crazy, one and all.

As it happened, Aggie's great-grandfather had been born a Crackleton before being adopted into the wealthy Hoople family – but that was another story in itself. She didn't advertise the connection.

Inside the house, Aggie encountered Police Chief Harry Teague sitting on the sofa across from Birdie Longstreet. He was a square-jawed man with a touch of gray in his neatly-combed hair. He wore a tan store-bought suit with a loosely knotted necktie over a white shirt. "Don't worry, Aggie," he said. "I waited for you to get here before questioning Birdie."

"Thanks, Harry."

"Your dad told me you were on your way over. Birdie asked for you."

"Has Birdie said what happened?"

The old lady didn't seem to notice they were talking about her. She sat there contentedly on the love seat, knitting what appeared to be a sweater.

"She hasn't said much. Only that she shot a spy. Called it her patriotic duty. Looks like she plugged poor ol' Fritz while he was putting mail in her box by the front door."

"Is that right, Birdie?" she turned to her client.

"Yes, my dear," the old woman looked up from her knitting. "That's the long and short of it. Would you like some tea?"

"No, thank you. I just had coffee with my friend Sissy."

"Oh, that's Barack Obama's granddaughter, right?"

"No ma'am. I think you are confusing former President Obama with Buckley Jackson, who lives here in Caruthers Corners. I believe President Obama lives in Washington, DC."

"Oh."

Aggie settled herself next to Birdie on the love seat. "Are you aware that the person you shot was the local mailman?"

The old woman leaned forward to squint at Aggie. "Fritz Berber, a mailman – ha! That's just what he wanted us to think. Delivering the mail was part of his spy routine. He read all our letters, you know."

"Maybe he was just nosey."

"Fritz Barber was a spy – what they call an agent in place. He worked for the Knights of the Roundtable."

"Birdie," corrected Harry Teague, "the Knight of the Roundtable was King Arthur's court. You know, Camelot and Sir Lancelot and men in tin suits."

"That's just where they got the name," insisted the old woman. "Fritz was a sneaky undercover spy, not a knight in shining armor."

"Did Fritz Berber threaten you, attack you, have a weapon?" prompted Aggie, taking notes on a yellow legal pad with a Bic ballpoint pen.

"No, no. I struck first. Shot him before he could put a bomb in my mailbox."

"Ma'am, we haven't found a bomb," said the Police Chief. "We've looked through Fritz's mail bag, patted him down, checked the shrubbery beside your front door – nada. No bomb, no weapons. Just scattered mail."

"Probably the bomb was set to self-destruct."

"No, I don't think so," Chief Teague gently replied. "There was no sign of an explosion, no sign of anything untoward."

"I saw him coming up the walk," she replied. "Knew I had to move quick. Easier said than done with my arthritis. But I got Gordie's gun, the one the Army returned with his personal effects, and made it to the front door just as he was lifting the flap to my mailbox."

"Then what happened?" asked Teague.

"I pushed open the door and pointed the gun at him. He said, 'What's that in your hand, Birdie?' And I answered, 'It's

Gordie's old pistol. Gonna have to shoot you, Fritz.' He said, 'Why's that, Birdie?' I told him, 'It's the only way to stop you,' and I pulled the trigger. Took some effort, but it went off with a loud *boom*! and Fritz fell over backwards into my azaleas with a hole in his forehead. Made me think of those Indian fakirs with their third eye."

Aggie knew she should have been counseling her client not to speak, but she was as fascinated by Birdie's story as Chief Teague was. Spies? Knights of the Roundtable? Birdie Longstreet was known for her confusing tales and unsubstantiated sightings, but this one was a doozy.

~ ~ ~

Randolph "Three Eyes" Johnson was a member of the infamous Crackleton clan, those ne'er-do-wells who lived just north of town. A collection of shacks, house trailers, a used car lot, and a squarish concrete-block convenience store. The Crackletons were known for their consanguinity. Their inbreeding had produced such oddities as giants, dwarfs, ectrodactyl-handed lobster boys, a hypertrichotic wolfman, microcephalic pinheads, even conjoined twins.

Three Eyes was an example of what's known as a "vanishing twin." His fetus had absorbed his twin brother while in the womb, the only remnant being an extra eyeball in the middle of his forehead. He called his nonexistent twin "Rex."

Having no job and lots of time on his hands, Three Eyes liked to go dumpster diving, poking around in people's trash cans for whatever he might find. He said it was one of Rex's favorite pastimes. They had found lots of interesting stuff – valuable jewelry, shorted-out electric hairdryers, a working vacuum cleaner, usable clothing, various pots and pans, sometimes money (spare change mostly). And, of course, food. People threw out a lot of perfectly delicious food.

Three Eyes ate well.

Earlier that day, he and Rex had been poking in Doc Medford's trash. Doc sometimes threw out pill bottles that still had one or two tablets inside them. That could offer some good tripping. Rex didn't particularly like drugs, but he had little say-so. Three Eyes controlled the arms and hands and such. Rex was what's called a parasitic twin, dependent on his host.

Anyway, Randolph and his brother Rex were sorting through Doc's trash bin. That was when they heard a loud *Thump! Thump! Thump*! The sound came from nearby, maybe over in that old Longstreet woman's yard.

Three Eyes and Rex stepped through a gate and peeked around the corner of the house. What they saw was beyond belief.

# CHAPTER THREE

## The Mail Is Going to Be Late

N'yen Madison was hunched over his souped-up Digital Storm computer workstation in his home office, working on a story about the Voyager I and II space probes. Despite being launched in 1977 to study the outer Solar System and interstellar space beyond the Sun's heliosphere, the two spacecraft were still sending back signals. This after doing flybys of Jupiter, Saturn, and the moon Titan, as well as Uranus and Neptune. All this had been accomplished with less computing power than found in the lock fob that opens the door on your car.

What made Voyager I and II interesting was that the probes were now about 17 billion miles from earth and like a Timex they keep on ticking. *Scientific American* wanted at 2,000-word piece for issue after next.

Just then, N'yen's wife phoned. He glanced at the oval clock on the wall: Its hands indicated 3:47 p.m. She was still on duty at the library. Sissy worked 9 a.m. to 5 p.m. Her assistant overlapped noon to 8 p.m. on weekdays. There was another team for weekends.

"Hi, Sugar Plum," he answered the phone.

"Hot news, Boy Toy. Word is, Birdie Longstreet shot a prowler. Aggie is going to defend the old loon."

"A prowler? Or was it a gnome yard sculpture? With Birdie, you can never tell."

"Somebody is dead. I just don't know who yet. Aggie promised to call the minute she gets a chance."

"Call me when you hear."

"You got it, Cutie Pie."

~ ~ ~

Lizzie Ridenour called her friend Maddy. "Mail seems to be late today. Have you got yours?"

"No," said Maddy. "Fritz seems to be behind schedule."

"Shucks, I was waiting for an Amazon delivery. I ordered a book, *The History of Quiltmaking in Indiana*. It was written by that idiot Holly Eberhart. I thought it might be worth a laugh." Around here, the post office delivered most Amazon packages.

"I didn't know Holly Eberhart had written a book." Holly had been the Indiana State quilting champion before Lizzie took the crown. "But if anybody knows the history, it's her."

"Hey, I know as much quilting history as Miss Holier-Than-Thou Holly."

"Yes, Dear Heart, but you didn't write a book."

Lizzie snorted. "*Hmmpf*, maybe I will."

~ ~ ~

"How you feelin'?" Myrtle Dobbler called back toward the jail cells.

"Better," came Tommy Truehart's feeble reply. The deputy slowly sat up from the cot, wiping the sweat from his brow with a handkerchief. "What's happening?"

"Haven't heard anything from the Chief. But just got a 911 call, if you're up to answering it. Lydia Lazynski reported a burglar."

"In the daytime?"

"I'm just the dispatcher. I don't know nothin' about criminal behavior," grumbled Myrtle.

"Lydia Lazynski – isn't she the mother of that famous quiltmaking champion?"

"That's right, Holly Eberhart's mom. Holly lives down in Indianapolis, but Lydia still lives here in town."

"Yeah, I know where she lives."

"So, you've got it?'

"Okay," he groaned, "I'm on my way. But I can't imagine what Lydia Lazynski has that a burglar would want to steal."

The cousin of a disgraced former mayor, Lydia had been arrested for stealing an antique quilt several years back. Pardoned by the governor, thanks to her daughter's intervention, Lydia had moved to a small cottage in the lower-income Melon Hill section of town. She lived on Social Security and a small stipend from her daughter, who fortunately had hooked onto a wealthy husband third time around. Holly still used the Eberhart last name of her first husband, but her latest hubby was a Pfizer. That meant Holly was Scrooge-McDuck-rich, practically wallowing in money.

Tommy Truehart hobbled out to his police cruiser and fired it up. Still feeling lightheaded, he decided not to use the siren or flashing lights. His system wasn't up to the commotion. He drove at 15 MPH and avoided potholes. Easy does it, he told himself.

On his way to Lydia Lazynski's, Deputy Truehart passed by Birdie Longstreet's house on North Main. The Chief's cruiser was angled in the driveway; Gus Bentley's cruiser was parked on the street. He recognized Aggie Madison's little yellow Kia sitting directly behind Gus's Chevy Tahoe. Guess they hadn't cleaned up the mess at Birdie's yet.

Good that the Chief had released him from the crime scene. Dead bodies were not Tommy's thing. He had what his mother called "a weak stomach."

Melon Hill was a rat's nest of small streets, a neighborhood that's easy to get lost in, but Tommy found the Lazynski house on his first try. Nothing looked untoward from the outside. But he was met by a hysterical woman when he knocked on the door.

"Thank goodness, you're here, officer. Somebody tried to break into my house. An awful looking man wearing a Halloween mask. I'm still shaking."

"Where did he go?"

"Nowhere. He's still here."

"Still here?" He drew his service pistol.

"Out back in my garden shed. I locked him inside while he was going through my trash bin. He's been beating on the door, demanding I let him out. But I called 911 instead."

"Mind leading me around back?"

"This way," she beckoned, taking an uneven slate path that circled the house.

The backyard was a pigsty, filled with broken lounge chairs, tread-worn tires, empty paint buckets, even tan asphalt tiles that had blown off the roof of the Lazynsky house. Melon Hill was not gentrifying fast enough, Tommy told himself as he took a position to one side of the bolted shed door. "Police!" he shouted, unsnapping the lock and kicking the door open. "Come out with your hands in the air."

"Don't shoot," came a voice from the darkened shed. "We was just checking out the trash. Nothing more'n that."

"Step outside, please," instructed the deputy, his Sig Saur pointed at the open shed door. "Nobody has to get hurt."

Three Eyes Johnson shuffled into the afternoon sunlight, all three eyes squinting at the brightness. "Tommy Truehart, you know me," he muttered. "Me and Rex were just making our rounds, dumpster diving. It's a hobby of ours." He held up a toaster. "Can you believe this woman was throwing away a perfectly good electronic device?"

"It burns the bread," Lydia Lazynsky said defensively.

"Ma'am, this ain't no burglar," Tommy assured her. "Just one of them Looney Tunes from Crackleton Corners. Three Eyes Johnson – he's perfectly harmless."

"What's he doing in my trash?"

The deputy holstered his pistol. "Just poking around. Nothing there you didn't intend to throw away, so you can't say he was stealing anything. But I can charge him with trespass, if you want."

"No, no. Let him go. It's just that he gave me such a fright. I thought that was a Halloween mask he was wearing, but I can see he's just one of them Crackleton freaks."

"Don't go disparaging my family," protested Three Eyes. Still blinking in the bright sunlight. "I ain't never been in jail like you have."

"Now see here –" Lydia sputtered.

"C'mon, Three Eyes, time to go," Tommy ushered the little man toward the front yard. "Best quit while you're ahead of the game. You and Rex want to maintain your record of never seeing the inside of a jail, don't you?"

"Can I keep this toaster?"

"Sure, why not? She threw it away."

# CHAPTER FOUR

## Something Strange

"I seed something strange today," said Three Eyes Johnson as he stepped out of the police cruiser. Deputy Truehart had given him a lift to Crackleton Crossing. Randolph and Rex lived with their sister, a microcephalic (a pinhead, in carny terms) known as Babs.

"Strange?"

"That's right. I seed an angel."

That gave Tommy pause. Although a member of Pleasant Meadows Baptist Church, he was not particularly religious in his outlook. "An angel, you say?"

"That's right."

"You mean an otherworldly being with wings and a halo?"

"I didn't see no halo."

Tommy Truehart turned off the engine and stepped out of the vehicle. "Where did you see this heavenly messenger?"

"In Miss Birdie Longstreet's front yard. Just this afternoon."

"Was the Police Chief there?"

"Didn't see him. But there were two police cars and that lawyer girl's car parked out front. I figured they were in the house with Miss Birdie."

Tommy took his cap off to scratch his head. "And you saw an angel standing outside the house?"

Three Eyes nodded. "Glowing with a heavenly eminence."

"Did this angel commit any crime?"

"Not that I saw. I figured it was the ascendant divine presence of Fritz Berber."

"Fritz?"

Three Eyes blinked rapidly – all three eyes. "You know, the mailman. The person Miss Birdie shot."

"How do you know she shot Fritz Berber?"

"Saw her do it."

Tommy was the one to blink now. "You're an eyewitness?"

"Guess you could say that. I was dumpster diving when I heard a loud commotion. When I peeked around the corner of the house, I seed the mailman trying to break down Miss Birdie's front door. He'd lost his mind, it seemed to me. Trying to force his way inside. She had no choice but shoot him dead."

~ ~ ~

Sissy gathered up her Hermès clutch purse and car keys, said goodnight to her assistant, and made her way to the cramped parking lot. Space was at a premium here atop the hill where the Perricock Museum of Science and History sat. Carefully, she guided her Electric Blue Nissan Sentra down the steep drive that led straight to Melon Rind House, where she and N'yen lived. The former home of Rita Rutaberger, they had bought it when Rita moved into the Hoople Retirement Center last year.

As Sissy turned into the driveway, she was surprised to find the front door wide open. That was odd. N'yen was fussy about locking up the house while he was working, sequestered in his fancy home office. He didn't like interruptions – unplugging the phone, disconnecting the doorbell, wearing earbuds to silence his surroundings. Fortunately for Sissy, he had a separate phone line for her calls. She was the only one who had that number (other than his Grampy).

Clambering out of the car, she rushed inside, calling out N'yen's name. But no answer. She noted that the living room had been ransacked. Pictures askew. Couch cushions tossed about. Cadenza drawers open. What had happened here?

Through the archway leading into the dining room, she could see the glass doors of the China cabinet gaping wide open, her silver punch bowl (a wedding gift) missing. The 65" TV in the den was missing too.

A burglary.

But where was her husband?

# CHAPTER FIVE

### Wanna Bet?

The dispatcher looked up as Chief Teague entered the squad room. "Where's the prisoner?" she asked.

"Birdie, you mean? Released her on her own cognizance," he replied. "She's not exactly a flight risk. I'm not sure she's ever been outside the city limits in all her life."

"That's probably a true fact."

"Say, Myrtle, where's Deputy Truehart?"

"I ain't Myrtle. I'm Elvina. There was a shift change while you was out."

"Sorry, I still can't get the hang of telling you two apart."

"Our mama still has trouble too."

"Do tell."

"You was asking 'bout Tommy. He's waitin' for you in your office."

"Didn't see his cruiser."

"Parked it around back, I 'spect. Shade of that oak tree keeps it cooler, he says."

"No wonder his cruiser's always covered in bird doo-doo. That tree is full of sparrows."

"That's why Maisie Walters' tomcat hangs out back there. He's quite a hunter."

Harry Teague hung his cap on the coat rack near the door. "What's Tommy doing in my office?"

"Got some big news for you. He turned up a witness to your murder."

"Oh? We don't really need a witness. Birdie confessed to shooting Fritz Berber. Open and shut. Case closed."

Elvina frowned. "Now don't you go bustin' Tommy's bubble. He's like the cat that dragged in a mouse. Pretend you like it."

"Yes, ma'am," he replied. But under his breath he muttered, "More like a cat that dragged in a white-throated sparrow."

"What was that?"

"Nothing."

The Chief strolled toward his office, only a few steps away in this pocket-sized police station. There had been a proposal to enlarge the building, add more jail cells, but the Town Counsel kept turning the request down. Not enough crime to justify the expenditure, they argued.

Deputy Tommy Truehart was slouched in the captain's chair that faced the Chief's desk. "Got a big breakthrough in the Birdie Longstreet murder case," he announced proudly, a wide smile slicing his face like a Jack O' Lantern. "Turned up an eyewitness who saw the whole thing."

"Who might that be?" asked Harry Teague, settling into his padded office chair. He resisted the impulse to shuffle through his mail. The police department got a morning delivery, so today's mail hadn't been disrupted by Fritz Berber's untimely demise. Tomorrow would be another story.

"Randolph Johnson."

"Three Eyes?"

"One and the same. He was checking out the trash at Mrs. Longstreet's house when he heard a banging on her door and stuck his head around the corner to investigate. Saw everything."

"Everything?"

The Deputy nodded. "Said Fritz was trying to break down the door. Said he saw Mrs. Longstreet shoot Fritz."

Harry nodded to encourage Tommy to continue. Getting a verbal report out of the deputy was a rarity, the boy being more comfortable with the solitude of web surfing on a computer. Even today, Beelzebub666 (that was Tommy's online handle) played Tower Duel games with N'yen Madison. He had a knack for technical things.

"Why don't you have Three Eyes come in and give us a sworn statement. We'll give a copy to the DA over in Burbyville. Don't forget to send one to Aggie Tidemore too. She's representing Birdie."

Tommy Truehart perked up. "Now that'll be an interesting sight t' see – the court trial. This'll be Aggie's first murder case. Ain't no way she's gonna get Mrs. Longstreet outta this pickle. Five will get you ten, she can't save Birdie from a guilty verdict."

Elvina's deep voice came wafting in from her switchboard station in the next room. "I'll take that bet. I 'spect that girl inherited some lawyering talent from her daddy. Back when he worked for a big law firm in LA, they called him Mark the Shark."

Deputy Truehart chuckled, kind of a *heh-heh-heh.* "We'll see who's the hammerhead in this case."

"You wouldn't wanna put thirty dollars on the outcome of this, would you, Tommy?" taunted the dispatcher. "Baby needs a new pair o' party shoes."

~ ~ ~

Dr. Franklin Delano Medford wasted no time getting to the autopsy on the dead mailman. State law required an autopsy on all homicides. And a bullet to the head certainly qualified as that.

There hadn't been many deaths in Caruthers Corners lately – homicide or otherwise. Even Yost & Yost was complaining about the lack of business. This was a statistical anomaly, for the town usually had a scattering of heart attacks and strokes (too many fried pork tenderloins in Doc's opinion) as well as farming accidents (tractors and hay bailers could be dangerous).

None of this had anything to do with Fritz Berber. Cause of death was pretty obvious, that third eye in the middle of his forehead, created by a 45-caliber slug from Birdie Longstreet's war-souvenir pistol. But having the extra time, Doc poked around in the usual places, weighing organs, inspecting the heart, examining the stomach contents. Gruesome stuff, unless you're used to it.

Aside from being coroner, Doc Medford was a general practitioner with added specialties in oncology and radiology as well as podiatry and reflexology. Doc was also a certified forensic pathologist. That's why he noticed a strange sticky substance in Berber's lungs. A few quick tests identified it as Dichlorodiphenyltrichloroethane, commonly known as DDT. It is a colorless, tasteless, and almost odorless crystalline chemical compound originally developed as an insecticide. Highly toxic, DDT had been banned worldwide in 2004 from agricultural use under the Stockholm Convention on Persistent Organic Pollutants. The convention was ratified by more than 170 countries.

How did the mailman get a snoot full of DDT, he wondered as he stitched up the familiar Y-incision.

# CHAPTER SIX

## Reporting a Burglary

N'yem looked up from his computer screen as Sissy burst into the room. "What's up, Honey Bun?" he smiled in her direction.

"Are you all right?" she shrieked, her eyes wide with fear.

N'yen was bewildered by her excited state. "Sure I am," he replied. "Why do you ask?"

Sissy waved her arms like a windmill. "Because the house has been ransacked. TV's gone. Silver punch bowl's gone. Lord knows what else. I was worried you might've been hurt by the robbers."

"Me? No, I was working away on my article. I didn't hear a thing."

"That's because you had your office soundproofed."

He pouted. "You know I don't like distractions when I'm writing."

"Hurry up, call the police. Report the burglary."

"Uh, okay." He picked up his iPhone and tapped in the number of the Caruthers Corners Police Department. He knew it by heart, from when Uncle Jim had been the police chief.

"Hurry up," his wife urged. "The burglars may still be in the house."

"Hello, Myrtle?" Pause. "Oh, hello, Elvina. You two don't just look alike, you sound alike too. This is N'yen Madison over at the Melon Rind House at the foot of Hoople Hill. I want to report a break-in."

~ ~ ~

"Chief," the dispatcher called across the squad room to Harry Teague. "That was N'yen Madison, Maddy's grandson. Says his house has been burgled."

"When it rains, it pours," he muttered, reaching for his cap. "C'mon, Tommy. Let's roll."

"Where's Gus?" asked Elvina. It was her job to keep track of all the deputies, although there were only a few full-timers – Tommy and Gus and Bingly (the night guy).

"Gus is still over at Birdie's house. Watching out for her. She's a dithering mess."

"Did she say why she shot Fritz?"

"She said she shot him 'cause he was a spy. But that's just crazy talk. Apparently, she shot Fritz 'cause he was trying to break down her front door."

"Why would he do that?"

"Dunno. But the cracks on the wood panels and the broken lock bear it out. With a good lawyer, she'll probably walk."

"Aggie Tidemore's a good lawyer. Takes after her daddy," said the dispatcher.

"Got that impression. She's still there with her client. Keeping Gus at bay."

"Good for her. I'm rooting for Birdie. I liked Fritz all right ... and Birdie *is* mad as a Hatter ... but I can't believe the old girl would deliberately harm anybody without a good reason."

"Hey," said Tommy, "bet's off. I didn't know about the busted door."

"Too late," guffawed Elvina. "You oughta spotted that damage to the door when you was on the scene."

"But I was sick."

The dispatcher smirked. "Poor excuse. I'm betting Birdie's gonna walk."

"Ain't our call, Elvina," interceded the police chief. "We just arrest 'em, gather the evidence, then leave it to a jury."

She eyed her boss. "You ever been on a jury?"

"Naw. They never call law officers."

"I was once, back when I was a cosmetologist for Yost & Yost. I'd hate to leave my fate in the hands of twelve yokels whose names were drawn out of a hat."

"That's not exactly the process."

"Being on a jury is boring work. Some days I stayed home and sent Myrtle in my place."

"That's illegal, you know."

"Nobody noticed the difference. Besides, she's fairer minded than me. I believe in public executions for parking tickets."

"But you were just saying you hoped Birdie got off –"

"I've always been a tad inconsistent, you know that. Otherwise, you'd issue me a gun."

"A dispatcher doesn't need a weapon. Besides, you and Myrtle are the last people I'd want to see carrying a gun. You gals are way too hot-headed."

"True. My sister and me do have a temper. I'd have shot Fritz if he came banging my door down."

"That's the puzzling part. I can't imagine why he'd try to break down Birdie Longstreet's front door. He always had a cheerful hello for everybody. Not a mean bone in his body."

"What did Birdie say?"

"She said she opened the door and shot him while he was putting mail in her box."

"But what about the splintered wood?"

"Nobody ever said Birdie Longstreet was consistent."

~ ~ ~

"Gotta go," said Aggie, shoving her iPhone into her beaded purse. Sissy had just called to tell her about the break-in.

Miss Birdie looked surprised. "So soon? I thought we'd have tea."

"No time, I'm afraid. But the deputy here – Gus – will stay on a while to look after you."

"You promise to come back?"

"Of course. I'm your lawyer now. I'll be back to plan a legal strategy with you. We shall prevail."

"Thank you, my dear."

Aggie knew she could easily win this one with an insanity plea. Nobody would dispute that with Birdie Longstreet.

Hadn't she called out the fire department for "a major house fire" when it was just the neighbor across the street barbequing steaks?

Hadn't she claimed she saw a sea serpent in Green Scum Pond? Turned out to be a little green water snake.

And didn't she recently accuse Yost & Yost of trying to construct a Frankenstein's monster out of spare body parts? That had been Margie Yost, the funeral home's part-time cosmetologist, trying to beautify Jerry Jason Johnson, whose skull got cracked like an egg in a fatal car wreck. No telling how Birdie sighted Margie doing her reconstruction work, as there are no windows in the mortuary's backroom.

And only last week, Birdie reported seeing James Dean drive through town in his Porsche sportscar – the same one he died in back in 1955.

Birdie was certifiable.

But harmless.

Well, Fritz Berber might dispute that last part if he were around to do so.

# CHAPTER SEVEN

## Big Ed's Boys

Aggie beat the two policemen to her cousin N'yen's home by ten minutes. Melon Rind House was only four blocks from Miss Birdie's. Aggie had floored her little Kia, ignoring the town's 25 MPH speed limit. Parking behind Sissy's two-tone blue Nissan, she ran up the front steps to the veranda-like porch.

The front door was gaping wide open. Before rushing inside, she shouted, "It's me, Aggie. Don't shoot if you have Buck's M-16." Sissy's grandfather had brought the 5.56mm automatic rifle back from the Vietnam War as a souvenir. Slightly illegal to own, but who was checking? Most people in this part of Indiana were gun nuts.

"In here," came Sissy's reedy voice. "Ignore the mess. I don't want to touch anything till the police do their thing. Fingerprints and all."

"A burglary?"

"More like a home invasion – but nobody was home."

"I was home," N'yen weighed in. "But I was sequestered away in my home office, so they didn't know I was here."

"And N'yen didn't know the marauders were out here either," added Sissy. "His office is soundproofed. And he was wearing his ear buds."

"—I like to listen to classical music while I work," he explained.

Sissy continued unabetted. "This was a more of a grab-and-run. They didn't go through the whole house."

"Thank goodness everybody is safe."

Just then they heard the crunch of tires in the driveway as the two police cruisers pulled in. They weren't using lights or sirens.

"Cops," announced Aggie, turning toward the door. "C'mon in, gentlemen. Our hands are up."

"Aggie," Chief Teague nodded. "N'yen and Sissy. What's the problem here."

"Look around," Sissy waved at the disarray of her living room. "We've been robbed."

"Hmm, what's missing?"

"Nothing much. TV, silver punch bowl. No jewelry or money taken. They didn't get to the second floor."

"They? Was it more than one intruder?"

"Actually, we don't know," Sissy admitted. "We didn't see them ... or him."

Chief Teague glanced around the room. "We haven't had anything like this. Last burglary was when one of the Crackleton boys rifled the lockers at the high school. Ed Crackleton usually confines his teams to petty larceny – purse snatching and picking pockets."

"You think this was a Crackleton job?" asked Aggie.

"Be my first guess. No offense intended. I know you have Crackleton lineage. And my deputy Gus used to be one of Big Ed's criminal miscreants before he got adopted by the Bentleys."

"No offense taken."

"Tell you what, I'll take a ride up to Crackleton Crossing, talk to Big Ed. Maybe we can get your TV back, but I wouldn't hold out any great hope. I'd suggest getting a stronger front door and better locks installed. Maybe a burglar alarm. It can be wired directly to the dispatchers at the police department. We can be here in ten minutes flat. I timed it driving over."

"Anything else?" asked Sissy, taking all this down on her iPad.

"Maybe buy a dog. Not that a dog or an alarm will do much to protect you from a determined burglar, but thieves will often move on to a house with less deterrents."

"Aren't you gonna take fingerprints?" asked N'yen.

"Hardly worth the effort. Most of Ed Crackleton's boys are too young to be in the system. But we'll take a swipe at it."

"I'll dust the living room," volunteered Deputy Truehart. "If we pick up one of Big Ed's boys, we might get a match."

"Anything more on the Birdie Longstreet incident?" asked Aggie.

"Matter of fact, yes," said Chief Teague. "Tommy came up with a witness to the shooting – Three Eyes Johnson."

"He saw it?"

"Yeah," nodded Tommy. "He'd been in Birdie's backyard prowling through her trash."

"Did he have anything new?"

"Nothing sensible. Claimed he saw an angel."

"What?" exclaimed the Police Chief. "You didn't mention that."

"Didn't see no need. It's obviously crazy talk."

"Gives me enough to impeach him as a witness," shrugged Aggie. "Everybody knows the  Crackletons – with a few exceptions – are crazy as bedbugs."

"What kind of angel?" pressed the Chief.

"Are there more than one kind?" replied his Deputy.

"Guess that depends on who you ask. Archangels, fallen angels, guardian angels, they come in all varieties."

"Three Eyes said this was an ordinary angel, a mist of light shimmering around his celestial body, twin humps of wings, the usual."

Sissy screwed up her face to object. "I don't see how you can call an angel 'ordinary.' You don't see them every day."

"I've never seen one ever," interjected N'yen.

"You don't believe in Heaven," rejoined his wife.

"Hey, I spend practically every night looking up at the heavens. I'm an astrophysicist, after all."

"Not a practicing one."

"Not a practicing Christian either. I was born a Buddhist."

Chief Teague joined their bickering. "I'm a member of Pleasant Meadows Baptist Church, but can't say I've ever seen an angel either."

"Three Eyes Johnson is a nut job, thinking he's got a twin brother named Rex inside o' him," scoffed Tommy Truehart. "You can see why I didn't bother mentioning this angel business."

"Well, I don't think it was an angel that trashed my house and stole my TV," said N'yen.

"—and my silver punch bowl," added Sissy.

Aggie couldn't help but laugh. "You've never used that punch bowl and never would've."

"But it looked nice there in my China cabinet."

"True."

"Besides, *you* gave it to us as a wedding gift. That made it special."

"Thank you, Sissy."

The Police Chief turned to go. "Tommy, dust for prints and write up a report. We'll keep our eyes open for anybody pawning a silver punch bowl. I'll alert the Burpyville PD. It'll probably turn up at Barney Brown's Pawn Shop."

# CHAPTER EIGHT

### Rex Had Nothing to Say

Three Eyes Johnson wasn't religious. He'd never set foot inside a church. That's why he was surprised by his encounter with an angel.

This heavenly body had been tall, broad-shouldered, impressive. The google eyes seemed to be staring into another dimension. He'd seen the twin protuberances of wings over the angel's shoulders. He wondered how far they could extend. Were angels able to fly? He thought he might've known the answer if he had ever attended Sunday School classes.

He was surprised that Rex had nothing to say about this encounter with an angel. Technically, Rex couldn't speak, having no mouth. But he and Rex shared the same brain, so he usually knew what his twin was thinking.

He remembered the scene vividly, as if it had been seared onto his eyeballs – all three of them – the way that image of Christ had been burnt onto that Shroud of Turin. At the time, it looked as if the angel was chasing ol' Fritz Berber. Fritz had been pawing at Miss Birdie's door as if trying to get inside – attempting to escape this superlunary avenger.

What could Fritz have done that would have caused this messenger of God to come for him? Whatever it was, Miss

Birdie had helped Fritz along on his journey to the Kingdom of Heaven. That pistol had made a loud *ka-bam*!

"Whattaya takin' nonsense about heavenly creatures?" reprimanded Three Eye's father. Fatty Johnson stretched out on his couch, his obese form topping 400 pounds these days. "You ain't got a religious bone in your body. No cause for you t' be seeing angels."

"Couldn't help it. I peeked around the corner and there he was, shimmering in the afternoon sunlight. He was a glorious sight t' see."

"Well, I don't believe it," declared his mother. "Ain't no such thing as angels an' devils." Eating an apple, her extra set of teeth chewed up the fleshy fruit like a Veg-O-Matic. With a double set of choppers, Freida Johnson was a freak in her own right.

"Hope I don't see no devil."

"Quit telling people you seen an angel or they'll drag you off to the looney bin," his mother warned. "People think we Crackletons are – how do they put it? – 'cuckoo for Coco Puffs.' You an' Rex just fuel that fire."

"Aw, shucks. I jus' know what I seed. But if you don't want me to repeat the story, I won't."

~ ~ ~

"Hey, Randolph, seen any angels lately," Jeb Crackleton greeted him as he walked into the convenience store. His great uncle was the local loan shark. At nearly 7-feet tall, Jeb was also a giant.

"Nobody's s'posed t' know about that angel I seed," pouted Three Eyes. "Mama said I have t' keep it a secret."

"Ever'body knows," said Faith Ann, Jeb's sister. She ran the convenience store. "You know you can't keep no secrets here at the Crossing."

"Mama's gonna be mad. Said I was gonna get sent to the looney bin. Rex says he don't wanna go there. He's shy, you know."

"He ain't no more than a stray eyeball," snorted Jeb. He was known to be mean-spirited. Few people liked him.

"Ain't so. Rex don't like you, Uncle Jeb. Neither do I."

"Breaks my heart," the tall man laughed. "You'd probably be better off in a looney bin."

"Got a question for you."

Jeb eyed his nephew warily. "Yeah?"

"What could Fritz Berber have done that would make an angel chase him?"

"Who knows? Steal his golden harp."

"I don't think he had a harp. He was carrying a long tube with a nozzle."

Faith Ann cocked her head. "Why would an angel have a rubber hose with a nozzle? That don't make no sense. Maybe you *do* belong in a looney bin, Randolph."

~ ~ ~

Three Eyes bought two candy bars for lunch. Payday was his favorite. He liked the peanuts. They had protein, he'd been told. Proteins were one of the main food groups for better health. He had a responsibility to take care of his body for Rex's sake.

As he made his way down Fourth Street that afternoon, looking for more trash bins to scope out, he spotted an olive-skinned woman sweeping off her front porch. Judging from the stack of cardboard packing boxes in her driveway, she had just moved in. At any rate, he didn't recognize her, so she must be new to these parts. Having grown up here, Three Eyes knew most everyone in town.

The newcomer nodded to him. "A pleasant day," she greeted him. That's when he noticed that she – just like him – had an eye in the center of her forehead. That stopped him in his tracks.

"Hello," he returned the greeting. "I notice you have a twin also."

"A twin?" She looked confused. Glancing at him more closely, she exclaimed, "*Phaya*! I thought you were a Hindu. But that's not a *bindi*."

"A what?"

"A painted dot on your forehead. What you have is, uh, a real eye."

"Yessum. Ain't yours real?"

The woman looked cross-eyed, as if trying to examine her own dot over her brown eyes. "No, this is what we call a *bindi*, a decorative mark worn in the middle of the forehead by Hindu women."

"My extra eye belongs to Rex, my twin brother. When we was born, he didn't come out on his own. He was a part o' me. His eye is all that shows."

"Oh. That is most strange."

"You say you're a Hindu?"

"Yes. I'm from India, a city called Ahmedabad in the western state of Gujarati. My name is Adivaita Nelson. But you may call me Addy, if you like."

"You say you're from India? What are you doing all way over here in Caruthers Corners?"

"My husband and I just moved here. Benny is the new manager of the retirement home up there on the hill."

"Benny Nelson – he don't sound Indian."

"He's not. We met when he was in the military, assigned to the US Consulate in Mumbai."

"What did you call that painted dot on your forehead?"

"A *bindi*. It represents a third eye, sometimes called the Eye of Wisdom. In Hinduism, the *bindi* is associated with the *ajna chakra*, the unconscious mind. The third eye is said to connect people to their intuition, help them receive messages from the past and the future."

"Like a fortune teller?"

"Not exactly."

"Eye of Wisdom? I oughta have a lot of wisdom being that my extra eye is for real."

# CHAPTER NINE

### Just Fishin'

Beauregard Madison IV was, as usual, out on the Wabash in the shallow-draft fishing boat that he co-owned with his pal Edgar Ridenour. They spent a good deal of their time dipping their baited hooks in the muddy waters. The Monster lurked somewhere in the river south of the Highway 201 Bridge. First one to land the fish would win a steak dinner from the other. That was the deal. There was a new restaurant down in Pitsville – Porterhouse Place, it was called – that TripAdvisor gave four stars for its charcoal steaks.

"Pull over to the shore for a minute," said Beau. "I gotta water the vegetation." Peeing over the side of the boat might alert that elusive largemouth bass to human proximity.

"Hold on, hold on," replied Edgar, goosing the motor to move the boat toward the shore. The fish were used to boats on the river. The Wabash used to be a major transportation route, but now it was shallow and silty, nearly impossible to pass in some spots.

The undergrowth along the shore was thick, like a knot of twine, but Beau pushed his way through, coming out at a sideroad on the north side of the river. From here, he could see Bobby Ray Purdue's glass-and-metal mansion out there in the middle of a vast watermelon field. Bobby Ray was one of the richest guys in northern Indiana, something of a minor league Elon Musk, investing in lots of big-boy toys – like online startups and gaming companies and motorcycle dealerships.

Matter of fact, wasn't that Bobby Ray himself out there behind his house digging a hole under a big willow tree?

Beau squinted his eyes to see better. Too bad he didn't have his binoculars with him. Looked like the home-grown zillionaire was burying something – a dead pet? a treasure chest? Trash compost? What could it be?

After Beau took care of business and found his way back to the waiting boat, he shared what he'd seen with Edgar Ridenour. These days, with his face covered by a shaggy beard, Edgar looked more like Grizzly Adams than a dapper bank president. His clothing – "my fishing duds," he described them – appeared as if he'd been living in them for the past month. Which was partially true. He'd pretty much given up showering. He was the complete opposite of his wife Lizzie, an attractive redhead who was stylish and well-coiffured, every hair in place.

"What do you think Bobby Ray was doing – burying a dead body?" mused Edgar.

"Naw, I doubt that," laughed Beau. "He would hire somebody to do that kind of dirty work. But he's sure got my curiosity aroused."

~ ~ ~

Cookie Bentley owned the watermelon fields surrounding Bobby Ray's mansion. He'd been trying to buy the land from her husband before he passed away. Bobby Ray wanted to assure his privacy. He had offered triple the land's value, but it was a no-go. He was very frustrated with Cookie.

That's why Aggie was surprised when she got a voice mail from her client saying, "I've decided to sell my two hundred acres north of the river to Bobby Ray Purdue. Draw up the papers. I'm letting him have it for the appraised value, though he's offered me many times more than that. But no need to be greedy, right?"

There was a sharp *beep!* then the message ended as abruptly as it began.

"Well, I wonder what brought that on," mused Aggie. Not that she was asking any questions. This transaction was the only thing she had going, other than the Birdie Longstreet murder case.

She knew Bobby Ray Purdue used some big law firm down in Indianapolis – Greasley Greasley & Beasley, or something like that. She checked her computerized contact list. There it was, an attorney named Walter Grisham, a partner at Grisham Grisham & Bartholomew.

GG&B – she'd been close, Aggie told herself. She had not dealt with many big white-shoe law firms yet and still had trouble getting the names right.

Aggie put in a call but was told that Walter Grisham was out of the office today.

She left her number.

What had made her Aunt Cookie change her mind about selling? she wondered. She certainly didn't need the money.

All her grandmother's friends were honorary aunts and uncles to her. These aunts – along with her Grammy –had made up the Quilters Club. She missed being a junior member of that quasi detective agency masquerading as a quilting bee. Too bad they had closed it down, just as she was getting old enough to be a full-fledged member.

~ ~ ~

"Burying something?" exclaimed Maddy Madison. "Like what?"

"Beats me," shrugged Beau. "I couldn't tell at that distance." He was having an early dinner, roast beef with watermelon sauce. One of his favorites.

Nobody had won that porterhouse steak today. The Monster still roamed the waters of the Wabash, uncaught. But that *status* wouldn't remain *quo* for long, Beau told himself. He had ordered a jig and pig – classic bait for largemouth bass. He'd gotten the idea from his grandson N'yen, the better fisherman among them.

"I throw a ½ ounce pork rind on a seven-foot heavy baitcasting setup with a 17-pound line when I'm pitching a jig," said his Vietnamese grandson. "Let the bait drop to the bottom, shake it, pick it up, and throw it back out there. I recommend using copolymer line because that's known for strength and abrasion resistance."

"Got it," Beau had nodded. A pig and jig – yep, this would be his secret weapon, a near-guarantee that Edgar would be buying him that juicy porterhouse steak.

"What could Bobby Ray have been burying?" pressed Maddy. You could see that it was worrying her worse than a hangnail. "It couldn't have been a dead pet. He's too narcissistic to own a cat or a dog. He'd be more likely to have a robot – and I don't mean an iRobot Roomba vacuum cleaner."

"You mean on like Rosey on *The Jetsons*?"

"More like Daryl Hannah in *Blade Runner*."

"Hmm, I get the difference."

"Don't you go getting any ideas, Beauregard Madison. You can confine your thoughts to the Roomba."

# CHAPTER TEN

## Date Night

Aggie Tidemore had a date. Since returning to Caruthers Corners, she had started seeing Bobby Elwood again. They had gone steady in high school.

Tonight, they were having dinner over in Burpyville, an Italian ristorante called Luigi's Casa del Buon Cibo. Aggie liked their Creamy Gnocchi with Bacon and Peas. Bobby liked the Chicken Cutlet with Spaghetti.

She hoped Bobby wouldn't drone on about work. He owned his own business, an exterminating company – Elwood's Bug Busters. She was tired of hearing about cockroaches and mosquitos and termites. He described killing pests with a little too much sadistic glee for her comfort.

Instead, tonight he was pumping her for details about Fritz Berber's murder. It was the talk of the county. Everybody had liked the mailman, although many agreed he was a little too nosey, always reading their letters and postcards as he made his rounds.

"You know I can't discuss it," she reminded him. "I'm representing the alleged murderer."

"Did Birdie do it? Word is, there was a witness."

"Randolph Johnson – how reliable do you think he will be?"

"Three Eyes? Wouldn't that additional eye make him all the better to see what happened?"

She was about to point out that Three Eyes was a Crackleton, a clan known for being loose with the truth. But, remembering her own lineage, she decided not to take that tact. "How's business?" she asked, deliberately stirring the conversation to a subject that bored her to tears. Better that – cockroaches and mosquitos and termites – than getting quizzed about the Fritz Berber murder.

"Doing great. The town's dealing with a bed bug infestation. I can hardly keep up. Had to hire a new man, a former Orkin guy from Fort Wayne. We've been working weekends too."

"What *are* bedbugs? All I know is that old admonition to 'sleep tight and don't let the bedbugs bite.' "

"You don't wanna be bit by bedbugs," he warned. "They're kinda like chiggers, but live in your mattress. Their bites produce pimple-like bumps with a dark red center. The itching will drive you crazy."

~ ~ ~

Later that night, when Aggie got home, she looked up bedbugs on Wikipedia:

> ***Cimex*** is a genus of insects in the family Cimicidae. *Cimex* species are ectoparasites that typically feed on the blood of birds and mammals. Two species, *Cimex lectularius* and *Cimex hemipterus*, are known as bedbugs and frequently feed on humans ... The insects are 3 to 9 millimeters (0.12 to 0.35 in) long and have flattened reddish-brown bodies with small nonfunctional wings.

"Ugh," she frowned. "Bloodsuckers."

She typed into the Google search box: How do you cure a bedbug bite?

The answer was disappointing:

> Bedbug bites don't usually need treatment, as they disappear on their own within a week or two. You might ease symptoms by using: A skin cream containing hydrocortisone (Cortaid) or an oral antihistamine such as diphenhydramine (Benadryl).

Okay, if there's no cure, maybe it *was* better to eradicate them in advance.

That was a good endorsement for Elwood's Bugs Busters, she thought. Sounds like her boyfriend would have steady work.

# CHAPTER ELEVEN

## Hollywood Squares

"It's driving me crazy," Maddy Madison said to the former members of the Quilters Club. "What could Bobby Ray Purdue have been burying out there in his backyard?"

Despite their retirement from amateur sleuthing, the four friends still met on Tuesday afternoons as usual – but these days by Zoom. Their visages – Maddy, Cookie, Lizzie, and Bootsie (now in Florida) – appeared in pixels on their computer screens, framed in little boxes like a miniature rendition of *Hollywood Squares*.

"Backyard?" hooted Cookie. "That's two-hundred acres of watermelon land. I ought to know. I own it."

"Maybe Bobby Ray was planting potatoes," suggested Bootsie. "His father was a farmer." Everybody knew Bobby Ray was her husband Jim's first cousin. Until Bobby Ray and his brother Newcombe amassed sudden wealth, the family had been dirt-poor tenant farmers.

"Potatoes," laughed Lizzie. "No way. If Bobby Ray wanted french fries, he'd buy himself a McDonald's franchise." Lizzie came from money – the Bergamachi banking fortune – so she knew about these things. Living a lavish lifestyle was her mantra. Bootsie and Jim were living mostly on Social Security these days, along with a small pension from his years as police chief.

"What about burying gold bars or silver coins – a hedge against a drop in the stock market?" suggested Maddy. But she was reaching.

"Or against a total monetary collapse," added Bootsie. Her husband was something of a world's-coming-to-an-end prepper, always worrying about an eminent apocalypse.

"That's not going to happen," chided Lizzie. "The economy is basically sound." She had confidence in the banking system. After all, her hubby Edgar Ridenour had been president of Caruthers Corners Savings & Loan.

"I've decided to sell Bobby Ray that two hundred acres," Cookie dropped the bombshell. "The paperwork's already in motion."

"But why?" asked Lizzie.

"His big ol' house is out there in the middle of that watermelon patch," smiled Cookie. "May as well give him some privacy. Assure him that no one can ever build a house next door. Give him space to plant potatoes, if that's what he wants."

"But I thought that land had a sentimental value to you," interjected Maddy. That particular plot was where Cookie's first husband, Bob Brown, had been killed in a freak tractor accident.

"Land is land," shrugged the tiny image of Cookie on the computer screen. "I'm thinking of selling it all off ... that is, what I have left."

"What you have left," scoffed her friend Bootsie. "You're still the largest landholder in Caruthers County!"

"Maybe so, but I don't need it. I'd rather spent my time quilting and making watermelon preserves than being a land baron."

"Baroness," corrected Maddy. She couldn't help herself.

"What brought all this on?" asked Lizzie. Surprised by her friend's unexpected reversal of attitude.

"Can't be a midlife crisis," teased Bootsie. "We're all pushing seventy."

"Call it a late-life crisis then," replied Cookie. "Gus doesn't want to manage the property. Not his thing. And I'm tired of doing it all by myself after I lost Ben." Ben Bentley had been gone some three years now.

"Well, it's yours to do with as you please," said Maddy, sensible as always. "But what about Bobby Ray burying something behind his house?"

"If you're so curious," jibed Cookie, "why don't you just go out there and dig it up."

"Maybe I will," said Maddy. But she didn't mean it.

~ ~ ~

Bobby Ray Purdue's house was a modernistic metal-and-glass structure that looked like something Frank Lloyd Wright might have designed after a few too many cocktails. But the famous architect had been dead for fifty years when Bobby Ray decided to build this "Fortress of Solitude," as he called it. A reference to *Superman* comic books. So, he'd hired an outfit out of Indy to draw up the plans. With its endless walls of windows, it was definitely a house where people who lived there should throw no stones.

The visible interior was cluttered with all kind of memorabilia – a genuine Tyrannosaurus skeleton from North Dakota; a World War I Fokker biplane; a stuffed Kodiak bear; dozens of neon-gurgling Wurlitzer jukeboxes; fifteen perfectly-restored Indian motorcycles; a world-class comic book collection; and every *Playboy* ever published, beginning with that first Marilyn Monroe centerfold issue – all those things that would give a pubescent youngster an orgasm. Having been one of the so-called Lost Boys – four local youths who disappeared into Never Ending Swamp only to turn up years later as members of a traveling circus – Bobby Ray was a prime example of arrested development.

When not satisfying his child-like impulses, he was a generous philanthropist, donating huge sums of money to worthy causes that benefited the town. The Haney Bros. Petting Zoo, the Circus Performers Retirement Home (now merged with the larger Hoople Retirement Center), the Strays & Others animal shelter, and lots more.

Bobby Ray always had a pretty girl on his arm. For a while he'd dated Tessie Humphrey (a real looker in her prime) but in recent years had moved on to movie stars and supermodels. With money, you could do that. You know, grab 'em by the … well, you get the idea.

His house was situated on an acre in the middle of one of Cookie Bentley's commercial watermelon fields. Her late husband Ben had sold the plot to him on impulse. Now Bobby Ray wished he'd bought the entire two-hundred acres.

After months of pestering her to sell the land, Cookie had given in, agreeing to let him buy the property for a pittance. Bobby Ray had been willing to pay through the nose (he could afford it), but she'd said that market value would be fine.

"I've got enough money," she told him. "So you can keep yours. Buy another elephant for the Haney Bros. Petting Zoo. Ol' Happy could use some company."

~ ~ ~

Addy Nelson liked Caruthers Corners. She had always dreamed of living in a small town, owning a pretty little house with twin gables and a white picket fence. And here she was, everything perfect, just as she imagined it would be.

Her husband liked his new job as director of the retirement center. The previous director – that British woman, Marybelle Olsen – had left everything in perfect order. As former manager of the Hoople Estate, Marybelle Olsen was more buttoned down than a naval commander's aide-de-camp. The Hoople Retirement Center ran with the precision of a well-tuned Big Ben clock.

Addy found the people here friendly –and interesting. She was thinking of that little man with three eyes. How unusual was that? All her life she had been surrounded by people with *bindi* – the third eye – but she'd never before encountered a real one!

Her husband's uncle – an old charlatan known as Professor McGuffey – was in the entertainment business, something to do with circuses as she understood it. He dealt with unusual people – midgets and giants and cojoined twins – but never to her knowledge a man with three eyes.

That reminded her, the Professor was coming to visit them this week. A stop-off before another Midwest tour. She'd better change the sheets in the guest bedroom. Nothing was more welcoming to a visitor than fresh sheets.

~ ~ ~

Deputy Gus Bentley kept his speed just under the posted limit as his cruiser zigzagged through the streets of Caruthers Corners. This was one of his thrice-daily patrols, ostensibly to be on the lookout for any crimes in progress, but in truth to reassure the populace of their safety by his presence.

Gus liked being a cop. As a kid he'd enjoyed playing cops and robbers – but being a Crackleton by birth, he had always rooted for the robbers.

He grew up stealing things, because that was the Crackleton way. Big Ed Crackleton ran a small-time ring of criminals, mainly youngsters adept at picking pockets and petty burglary. He'd been one of Big Ed's boys before he got adopted by the Bentleys. Now his life was different, walking the straight and narrow, a police officer.

But it was boooring.

# CHAPTER TWELVE

### Wasn't Us

**N**'yen was watering the patchy brown lawn in front of his house when he spotted Three Eyes Johnson sauntering down the sidewalk. Obviously up to no good. He had a sneaky look in his eyes (all three).

Gus Bentley had said his uncle – that latter-day Fagin, Ed Crackleton – sometimes used Three Eyes to scout for houses to burglarize. Even though Chief Teague denied there had been any recent burglaries or home invasions – other than N'yen's recent mishap – it was well-known that Big Ed's boys were ransacking local neighborhoods.

"Hey there, Randolph," called N'yen, stepping over the white fence that demarcated his property line. "Got a minute?"

"Hello, Mr. Madison," the freakish man replied. "How are you on his fine day?"

"Not so well. My house was burglarized yesterday. Sissy's very upset."

"Wasn't us," he replied without having to be asked. "I know you're adopted and all that – them slanty eyes are a clue – but you're Maddy Madison grandson, so that kinda makes you a Crackleton. And we don't steal from our own people."

"If the Crackletons didn't do it, who did?"

"Beats me. But I'll ask Big Ed if you want me to. He don't like other robbers working his territory. He'll know who did it."

~ ~ ~

Ed Crackleton had been branching out. Rather than turning his minions loose on Caruthers Corners, he had been shipping them out to Burpyville and Pitsville and Berne and Geneva – nearby towns that offered an easy commute.

One of Ed's sons, the owner of Bob's Autos, that used car lot at the Crossing, had provided a 16-seater Toyota Hiace commuter van for distributing the teams of juvenile pickpockets, purse snatchers, and grifters (all family members). The van was stolen; its license plates swapped; and the VIN number removed. But who was being picky? It ran well and got decent gas mileage.

Lately, they had been laying low on burglaries. Raised to be a farmer, Ed compared this tactic to that of rotating crops, a renewal practice that reduces the reliance on one set of nutrients.

That put Three Eyes out of work for a while, but he lived off a family stipend anyway. Crackleton Crossing operated like a commune, all the ill-gotten gains divided equally among its inhabitants.

Just as Three Eyes had thought, Big Ed's gang was not responsible for the invasion of N'yen Madison's house. It was a "protected zone" – family ties and all that.

But if the Crackletons didn't do it, who did?

Ed Crackleton vowed to punish the person or persons responsible for this incursion into his territory – once he found out just who was behind the deed.

~ ~ ~

Granny Crackleton – Ed's older sister and matriarch of the family – put out the word. There are no true secrets. It didn't take a full day to get back the answer, the name of the burglar. And the answer was indeed surprising!

# CHAPTER THIRTEEN

## Dichlorodiphenyltrichloroethane

Aggie was doing paperwork on the Birdie Longstreet case when she got an unexpected call from Doc Medford. Her practice was too new – and much too small – to have an assistant, or secretary, or receptionist, or paralegal. It was a one-man shop – or one-woman shop, Aggie corrected herself. So, she answered the phone with a harried "Hello?"

"Aggie, it's Doc here. Found something puzzling in my autopsy of Fritz Berber. Already told Chief Teague, so I thought I'd better give you a heads-up too."

"Found what?"

"The presence of dichlorodiphenyltrichloroethane in Fritz's lungs."

"Dichloro –?" she stumbled over the word. "What's that?"

"DDT."

"I thought the use of DDT had been banned."

"It has. That's why this whole thing is puzzling. I can't figure out where he would've breathed in a snoutful of that nasty chemical."

~ ~ ~

"Bobby, I've got a quick question about bedbugs."

"Don't tell me you've got them in your house?"

"No, nothing like that," said Aggie. "I've just been thinking about our conversation last night. You said the town was seeing an infestation of bedbugs."

"Right."

"Well, my question is how do you kill them?"

"Lots of ways. Heat will do the trick. But if you call Elwood's Bug Busters, we use special insecticides. Pyrethrins and pyrethroids are the two most common compounds used to control bedbugs and other indoor pests."

"Pyreth ... what?"

Bobby laughed. He liked knowing more about a subject than his snooty Yale-educated girlfriend. "Pyrethrins are botanical insecticides derived from chrysanthemums," he explained patronizingly.

"The flower?"

"Yep. But here at Bug Busters, we prefer to use pyrethroids, a synthetic chemical insecticide that acts just like pyrethrins. It's cheaper, but does just as good a job."

"Do either of these compounds contain DDT?"

"No way. DDT hasn't been used as a pesticide since 1972 – long before you or me were even born."

"Why not?"

"Back in the 1950s, DDT was the standard way to get rid of bedbugs, but it's not effective to use today and has risks."

"Not effective?"

"By the late '50s, many populations of bedbugs around the world had developed a resistance to DDT.

"And you said risks – what kind of risks?"

"DDT is considered a possible human carcinogen. And studies of laboratory animals have shown it affects the liver and reproduction organs. Dangerous stuff. Enough of it can kill you."

~ ~ ~

Aggie wasn't sure Bobby would make a good expert witness. He'd dropped out of University of Indiana in his sophomore year. Goodness knows what inspired him to get into the pest control business. It wasn't a difficult profession to break into. In Indiana, all you had to do was pass a two-day seminar that costs $200 ... or work under a licensed applicator for 90 days. The exam covers all aspects of pest control and pesticide application.

The final requirement is to either own a pest control business or work for a business that can apply for a license for you. Licenses cost $45 each.

Not much brainpower required.

Bobby was a sweetheart, but not very smart when it came down to it. She'd have to do a little digging herself.

So, after hanging up, she turned to Google again:

According to the National Pesticides Center, pyrethrins are low in toxicity to people and other mammals. However, if it does get on your skin, it can be irritating. This pesticide sometimes causes tingling or numbness at the site of contact.

However, DDT can be much worse: People excessively exposed to dichlorodiphenyltrichloroethane from working with the chemical often report a prickling sensation of the mouth, nausea, dizziness, confusion, headache, lethargy, incoordination, vomiting, fatigue, tremors in the extremities, anorexia, anemia, muscular weakness, hyperexcitability, anxiety, and nervous tension. DDT affects the nervous system by interfering with normal nerve impulses. It causes the nerve cells to repeatedly generate an impulse which accounts for the repetitive body tremors seen in exposed animals.

In 1948, the Journal of the American Medical Association reported a case of accidental fatal poisoning by ingestion of a commercial DDT preparation that came to autopsy six and one-half days after drinking the poison.

The United States Environmental Protection Agency categorizes DDT as a B2 carcinogen. This means DDT has been shown to cause cancer in laboratory animals, but there is no firm evidence that it causes cancer in humans.

DDT is an organochlorine insecticide that was first synthesized in 1874 by a German chemist named Othmar Zeidler. Later, in 1939, another scientist, Paul Müller, discovered DDT's insecticidal properties. DDT was initially used by the military in WW II to control malaria, typhus, body lice, and bubonic plague.

In addition to public health uses, farmers used DDT on a variety of food crops worldwide. Such agricultural products included beans, cotton, soybeans, sweet potatoes, peanuts, cabbage, tomatoes, cauliflower, brussels sprouts, and corn. DDT is highly persistent in the environment. The soil half-life for DDT is from 2 to 15 years.

Also, DDT was commonly used for pest control. From bedbug spray to a cockroach deterrent, the pesticide was common in the United States until banned by the EPA in 1972.

No longer used in agriculture. No longer used as a household pesticide. So, where did Fritz Berber get exposed to DDT?

# CHAPTER FOURTEEN

## A Mythological Deity

Addy Nelson met her husband for lunch at McDonald's. Ironically enough, McDonald's reminded her of home. Today, India has 512 McDonald's restaurants. Mickey D's is that country's second-largest fast-food chain in terms of revenue. She loved the Chicken Maharaja Mac. Respecting cultural sensitivities, McDonald's restaurants in India do not serve beef or pork products. Here in America, she made do with the familiar Filet-O-Fish or McChicken sandwich.

Addy and her hubby were physical opposites – she with her olive skin and *ajin* dot in the middle of her forehead, Benny with his ruddy face and carrot-red hair. But having lived in America for the past ten years, she was very acclimated to the Western culture. She no longer wore a *sari* or a *ghagra choli*; she preferred slacks and tank tops.

"Did I tell you about the interesting man I met?" she said to Benny as they munched on their crispy fish sandwiches and shoestring fries (supersized).

"What man?"

"A fellow with three eyes."

"Like you?"

"No, no. His third eye was real. He could see with it. I wondered if he might be a Tryambaka Deva."

"Like Lord Shiva?" Having been marred to Adivaita for 14 years, he was well-versed in Indian culture.

"No, this man is more gentle, a lost soul I think. Shiva is fearsome, the god of destruction. This fellow would not harm a fly."

"What's his name?"

"Randolph – Randolph Johnson."

Benny made a face. "Oh, that guy."

"What guy?"

"They call him 'Three Eyes.' He's a Crackleton."

Addy looked confused. "What's a Crackleton?"

"The Crackletons are a local family with a bad reputation. They are known for their lawlessness ... and for an array of deformities from inbreeding."

"Deformities? Do you consider an 'Eye of Wisdom' a deformity?"

"Sometimes, Dearest Heart, an eye is just an eye."

~ ~ ~

Randolph "Three Eyes" Johnson didn't feel like a mythological deity. Matter of fact, he barely felt human. It was difficult being different – although the Crackletons had learned to live with it, even profit from their aberrations. Many of them worked off and on for carnival sideshows.

Randolph's sister Babs made a good living as a "pinhead" in a number of traveling shows. Since joining McGuffey's Cabinet of Curiosities, she wasn't home much. That sideshow regularly toured the Midwest.

Phil Jinks, with his flipper-like appendages, had toured with Applerouth's Oddities & Rides for the past dozen years. He was a classic case of phocomelia. All his children shared the same lobster-claw attributes. They were guaranteed a good living with traveling carnivals and sideshows.

Then there was Abel and Abner Crackleton, conjoined twins attached at the hip. These freakish sons of Big Ed Crackleton were featured in the Baltimore Geographic Society's 1994 study of deformities in Crackleton Crossing.

When the Baltimore Geographic Society did a similar study of the Bahamian island of Spanish Wells, there was a great uprising where copies of the bound volumes were burned by the hundreds. To the contrary, everybody in Crackleton Crossing bought themselves a copy of this study with a misplaced sense of pride. Every home had a copy of the Baltimore Geographic Society study and the King James Bible – two indispensable additions to every bookshelf.

Randolph couldn't help but ruminate about the woman he'd met the other day, the one with three eyes. Sure, the middle one was painted on, but he could appreciate the kindred spirit. She'd said a third eye symbolized the power of knowledge, and the ability to detect evil. He wasn't sure about his knowledge, but he did feel like he could sometimes sniff out evil.

For instance, he had a strange feeling about that angel he'd encountered. The celestial being had seemed to emanate more evil than good. But, then again, didn't Rev. Pillsbury say the Devil himself was a fallen angel?

> Samael is a fallen archangel who was banished from Heaven by God after a failed rebellion, being sent to Hell as its new ruler and later changing his name to Lucifer.

As 2 Peter 2:4 put it:

> "For if God did not spare angels when they
> sinned, but cast them into Hell ..."

Maybe he'd met up with a bad angel?

# CHAPTER FIFTEEN

## The Whiz

**B**eing a computer whiz, Deputy Tommy Truehart did a background search on the dead mailman. What he found was unsettling. Most people thought of Fritz Berber as a friendly, but nosey *mensch*. Jewish, he was a member of the synagogue over in Burpyville. There wasn't one in Caruthers Corners.

Before joining the US Postal Service some twenty years ago, Berber had been in the military – but Tommy couldn't access his records. The query prompted a response that said CLASSIFIED – AUTHORIZED EYES ONLY.

Strange.

Tommy was not a Black Hat, but he was in fact a very skilled hacker. Nonetheless, no matter how hard he tried, he could not break through the fire wall that protected Major Fritz Rottweiler Berber's military records.

That was unusual. Tommy was good at this.

It wasn't that he needed the information to close out the homicide files, but more that it now provided a personal challenge. Try as he may, Beelzebub 666 could not get in. That sort of thing gnawed at him.

The only other hacker he knew as skilled as himself was N'yen Madison. For years they had played Tower Duel against each other. N'yen was a slightly better player, but Tommy refused to acknowledge that fact.

N'yen had entered Northwestern University on an Advanced Placement program, earning a PhD in Astrophysics while still in his teens. Now in his early 20s, he was a senior editor for *Scientific American*. But he still played online games with Tommy.

Tommy Truehart used an encrypted text to reach out to his young friend. N'yen always responded immediately to Tommy's messages like Bruce Wayne to a Bat Signal.

> WHAT'S UP, BEELZEBUB666?

> NEED YOUR SKILLS.

> HOW SO?

> CHECKING OUT FRITZ BERBER. CAN'T ACCESS HIS MILITARY RECORDS. CAN YOU?

> DOES A CHICKEN LAY EGGS? GIVE ME A HALF HOUR.

~ ~ ~

Ironically, living only miles apart, N'yen Madison had never met Tommy Truehart face-to-face, at least not in a social way. Sometimes they saw each other in passing (it was a small town) and nodded their hellos, but there had been no hanging out, no friendly chitchats, no personal interaction, as if their online relationship was separate from everyday life. They had proved to be worthy opponents in games like Tower Duel or XDefiant, earning a grudging admiration each for the other. But they had little else in common.

Everyone called N'yen a Brainiac, an accurate enough description. But sometimes Tommy, a homegrown lad, did not get his due. People acknowledged him as a tech wizard and hired him on the side to hook up their Internet or install burglar alarms or fix their on-the-fritz computers, but little did they know about his secret online life, roaming and romping through cyberspace. There were few databases he couldn't crack, few fire walls he couldn't breach, few passwords he couldn't uncrypt.

But whenever he hit a dead end, he turned to his little Vietnamese hacker buddy. There was a mutual respect between the two twentysomethings.

~ ~ ~

N'yen was back within fifteen minute.

> I GOT IN.

> WHAT DID YOU FIND?

> FRITZ BERBER IS NOT WHO WE THOUGHT HE WAS.

# CHAPTER SIXTEEN

## Aggie's Client Meeting

Birdie Longstreet's parlor looked like a scene out of *Meet Me in St. Louis*, a turn-of-the-past-century room filled with overstuffed sofas and faded lace doilies, Tiffany lamps and bric-a-brac cabinets lined with cutesy Hummel figurines. Her house smelled of lavender and old age.

Aggie sat across the coffee table from the elderly woman, as usual taking notes on a yellow legal pad. "Tell me, Mrs. Longstreet, when did you become aware that Fritz Berber was at your front door?"

The old lady screwed up her face as she tried to remember. "Well, I had been awaiting the mailman that morning. I was expecting a letter from my sister. She lives in Chicago, just off the Loop. The mail usually comes around noon. Fritz does the town first, then expands his rounds to the outer limits, the Bentley farm, Wabash Acres, places like that. But he seemed to be running late that day."

"So when did he come?"

"A little after noon. I'd been keeping an eye out for him. First thing I heard was a *bang-bang-bang* pounding at my front door and somebody shouting, 'Let me in, let me in right now!' That was Fritz, but he never knocks on the door, just drops my letters in the box or leaves any packages on the front mat. I was taken aback, to say the least."

"What did you do next?"

"Fearing it was some kind of home invasion, I got out my husband's gun, the one he carried in the Korean War. It's big and heavy and hard to shoot. Then, I looked through the peephole and saw that it really was Fritz, but he had gone berserk, throwing himself against the door, trying to break it down. You saw how the wood was splintered. Obviously, Fritz had lost his mind."

"Then what happened?"

"I told him to stand back or I would shoot. An elderly lady like me has to protect her honor. No telling what that madman had in mind. My virtue could have been at stake."

"Did he stand back?"

"No, the door gave way to his shoulder and I pulled the trigger. Had to use both hands. The explosion knocked me backward, landing me on the floor. My coccyx still hurts. Fritz grunted and fell backward onto he stoop. One look told me that he was dead as road kill. That's when I dialed 9-1-1 to report a home invasion."

"Did anyone see this?"

"Matter of fact, yes. There were a couple of passersby, but they didn't stick around. Skedaddled right away."

"Did you get a look at them?"

"Good enough. One was Three Eyes Johnson. The other was a Spaceman."

~ ~ ~

Three Eyes thought it must be more than a coincidence: that he had a third eye; his new friend Addy had three eyes; and Miss Birdie had given Fritz Berber a third eye by plugging him straight in the forehead with her trusty old forty-five.

Strange, that.

He ambled down the sidewalk toward Addy Nelson's house, hoping to see her again. Maybe she'd be working in her yard or sweeping her porch or getting the mail out of her box.

That gave him pause. Would there be any mail delivery with the mailman dead? Surely, they had a backup mailman, he told himself. The United States Post Office was a big business, with more that 600,000 postal employees, according to what he'd once read.

Randolph was an avid reader, but he and Rex did not share the same taste in books. Usually, while he read, Rex would shut his eye and go to sleep.

He could see the Nelson's stately Victorian just down the street. With its gabled roof and rounded towers, the three-story structure was typical of many houses hereabout. He could see a large truck parked in front of the Nelson residence. Was Addy moving away? He thought she had just moved in. Maybe her husband's job at the retirement home hadn't worked out.

That thought made him sad, losing his new friend only days after meeting her.

But wait – that wasn't a moving truck. The sign on its side proclaimed *McGuffey's Cabinet of Curiosities*. Wasn't that the roadshow his sister Babs toured with? What was that vehicle doing parked in front of Adivaita Nelson's house?

# CHAPTER SEVENTEEN

## The Man Who Didn't Exist

It was a historic first, N'yen Madison and Tommy Truehart meeting face-to-face. But they needed to discuss what the government website had been hiding about Fritz Berber.

Being cautious, they took a booth in the far corner of Cozy Café for privacy's sake. Even Maisie Walters kept her distance after serving them watermelon milkshakes, sensing the hush-hush nature of their meeting.

"So, what did you find out about Fritz Berber?" asked the young deputy, too excited to sip on his shake, blue eyes locked with N'yen's dark brown orbs.

"There is no Fritz Berber," came the cryptic response.

"Whattaya talking about?" Tommy frowned with obvious confusion. "Fritz Berber is the mailman Birdie Longstreet plugged straight between the eyes the other day."

"That was a man named Ivor Muscovy."

"No, that was Fritz Berber. I matched his prints to Post Office employment records. No question about it, that was ol' Fritz."

N'yen shook his head. "I'm telling you there is no Fritz Berber. That was merely an assumed name. He was really a Soviet defector, an MVD officer named Ivor Muscovy. He'd been relocated to Caruthers Corners under a federal witness protection program. New name, new life, new job. He blended in pretty well. He came here twenty years ago, claiming to be from upstate New York, the son of Holocaust survivors. But he was really a former major in the Ministry of Internal Affairs of the USSR."

"A Russian spy?"

"Kinda."

~ ~ ~

Sissy was reorganizing books on the reference shelf at the library. Browsing patrons frequently misplaced books, leaving them out of order. She came across a thick tome that she recognized without reading the title, the 1994 *Baltimore Geographic Society's Study of Deformities and Physical Aberrations from Consanguinity in Crackleton Crossing, Indiana.*

This volume was on the **DO NOT CHECK OUT** list, only available for researchers to access while inside the library. The reason being that copies of the study were quite rare. While practically everybody at Crackleton Crossing owned one, the book was long out of print, hard to replace.

Highly illustrated, the Baltimore Geographic Society's study was shocking to the faint of heart. Many people pictured in the book were still alive, still residing at the Crossing. Although genetically afflicted members (pinheads, conjoined twins, etc.) of the community stuck close to home, it was not unusual to encounter people with six fingers or lobster-claws in local shops or supermarkets.

Opening the thick leather-bound volume, Sissy noted an inscription on the flyleaf:

*To Randolph,*
*From your loving mother Freida*

This volume had once belonged to Three Eyes Johnson. Surprising that he had surrendered his own personal copy to the library's collection. Maybe he wasn't sentimental about his ancestry.

~ ~ ~

As N'yen and Tommy finished off their frothy watermelon milkshakes, the deputy said, "You won't believe what Three Eyes Johnson told me he saw."

"What? Elvis Presley buying a Big Red soda at the Crossing's convenience store?"

"Just about. Said he saw an angel."

"You mean like a dreamy looking female?"

"No, like Gabriel blowing his horn."

"He's getting as squirrely as his Uncle Claude." Claude Crackleton was a schizophrenic who was convinced an alien lived inside him. Not that much farther off the charts than Randolph and his vanishing twin brother Rex.

"Where did he see this apparition?"

"When Miss Birdie shot Fritz Berber ..."

"You mean Ivor Muscovy," corrected N'yen.

"Right," nodded Tommy. "I'm not sure what to make of that. Do you think it has anything to do with why he got shot?"

"Doubt it. Birdie Longstreet's connection with Russian spies doesn't go any farther than Boris and Natashia on *Rocky the Flying Squirrel* TV reruns."

"You may be wrong about that. I'm told she said Fritz was a spy belonging to an organization called the Knights of the Roundtable."

"Like in King Arthur?"

"No, just the same name. I'm going to try tracing them next."

# CHAPTER EIGHTEEN

## Say a Little Prayer

**S**unday Brunch was becoming a tradition for Aggie and her two best-est friends. Maybe it was a comment on the tenuous nature of her relationship with Bobby Elwood that she didn't include him on these weekend get-togethers. Today, the trio decided to try out a new restaurant down in Pitsville, a place called The Cliff, an eatery overlooking one of the area's large water-filled gravel pits.

Located just south of Caruthers Corners, Pitsville was a former mining town that was becoming artsy-fartsy, filled with art galleries and gift shops and fancy restaurants.

They shared the ride down in Aggie's little yellow Kia, N'yen taking the backseat and grumbling all the way. He and his cousin had bickered in a friendly way all of their life together. Sissy was the peacemaker, soothing ruffled feathers, acting as mediator in their lighthearted quarrels.

"I'll buy you a car with a bigger backseat," he offered. N'yen, like Aggie, had a healthy trust fund, their share of the Hoople fortune.

The Hoople Quadruplets had been famous in their time, the town's biggest celebrities. They had once even appeared on the cover of *Time* Magazine. By the time it was discovered they were not true quadruplets, their parents had amassed a huge fortune from public appearances, advertisements, endorsements, even one B-grade movie. When the Quads passed away, the last two of them going in a massive traffic accident, their fortunes had passed along to Maddy Madison and her fraternal twin sister, Maisie Walters.

Maddy had set up trust funds for all her children and grandchildren. Then she donated that big stone monolith atop Hoople Hill to the town as a retirement home (now managed by Benjamin Nelson) and moved with hubby Beau back to a stately Victorian on Melon Pickers Row.

By some accounts. Aggie and N'yen had spent more time with their grandparent growing up than with their own parents. As a result, they were more like siblings than cousins. And they squabbled like siblings, nothing serious, just silly things. They were truly quite fond of each other.

The Cliff offered a buffet brunch, more a smorgasbord, heavy on the salads and fruits, but with an omelet chef on duty. N'yen had two omelets despite his small size. He was still the diminutive 5-foot-2 he'd been since 12. His wife Sissy and cousin Aggie were a full head taller than N'yen, but they were careful never to wear high heels around him.

"Did you guys hear about Three Eyes Johnson seeing an angel?" he said just to be making conversation over brunch.

"An angel? Are you pulling my leg?" laughed Sissy. She had grown up in a very religious household, but that didn't extend to a belief in visitations from heavenly messengers with wings and harps.

"No, I heard it from Tommy Truehart. He interviewed Three Eyes after Miss Birdie offed the mailman. Three Eyes witnessed the whole shooting. Figured the angel he saw was that of Fritz Berber ascending into heaven."

"Wait a minute," Aggie stopped him. "Miss Birdie told *me* she saw a Spaceman."

"Angel, Spaceman, what's the difference? Three Eyes and Miss Birdie are both nuttier than a Claxton, Georgia, fruitcake."

"Miss Birdie may get confused about what she sees, but she usually sees *some*thing."

"Whatever," shrugged N'yen. "I'm only repeating what Tommy told me when we got together for milkshakes."

"You and Tommy got together?" repeated Sissy, the surprise evident in her voice. "I thought you guys only knew each other online."

"That was essentially true until yesterday."

"What brought you together – a new computer game?"

"No, we turned up something interesting about Fritz Berber."

"Hey," said Aggie. "I'm Miss Birdie's lawyer. Anything you and Tommy know about the alleged murder victim, you'd best tell me. Legally, I get to see everything as part of discovery."

"Doubt this had anything to do with Miss Birdie shooting him," said N'yen. "Tommy hasn't even told Chief Teague. But it's a doozy. Fritz Berber wasn't Fritz Berber. He was a Soviet defector hidden away under the auspices of a federal witness program."

"A spy?" said Sissy, practically spitting out her mouthful of omelet. "In Caruthers Corners?"

"Yeah, it's quite a mystery."

"Too bad the Quilters Club disbanded," sighed Sissy. "They would get to the bottom of this."

"Listen to you wimps," interjected Aggie. "We don't need the Quilters Club."

"Why not?"

"Because we three used to be junior members of the Quilters Club. Sissy and me still make patchwork quilts. We could figure this out."

"Do we want to do that again – play amateur sleuths?" frowned Sissy.

"We weren't playing," insisted Aggie. "We really did solve crimes."

N'yen shrugged. "I'm already involved, digging into this with Tommy. You might say I'm doing it at the request of the police. He's a deputy, you know."

"And I'm already involved," added Aggie. "Birdie Longstreet is my client and I have to defend her from a murder charge."

"That's going to be tricky," said N'yen. "She's already admitted shooting Fritz Berber. And there was an eyewitness. Maybe two eyewitnesses."

"Yes, but there may have been extenuating circumstances. Self-defense, for instance. Fritz Berber was trying to force his way into her house. What was that all about?"

"Maybe the debbil made him do it," Sissy offer her sarcasm.

"Hmm," said Aggie. "Maybe the angel made him do it."

"That's an interesting defense," N'yen rolled his eyes. "*Deus ex machina.* Blame it on God."

~ ~ ~

Rev. Phillip Pillsbury, minister of the First Presbyterian Church in Caruthers Corners, was hosting his ice cream sundae bar ("Sundaes on Sunday," he called it) after the morning's service. It was very popular with his congregation, spooning homemade watermelon ice cream as they rehashed the day's sermon. This along with the monthly "Spaghetti Western Night" (pasta and a cowboy movie) were great fundraisers for the church.

Three Eyes Johnson never missed either event. He could afford them, given his family allowance and money he got for the things he fished from people's trash. Soda bottles were plastic these days and virtually worthless, but he sometimes found good items to pawn or sell at flea markets. Rags, he sold by the pound once a month at a warehouse in Burpyville.

While Three Eyes didn't attend any church services, he enjoyed these social events. The congregation treated him ... almost normal. Long used to his presence, nobody screamed at the sight of him and his third eye; children didn't run away in fear; the congregation seemed to accept him as "one of God's children."

He liked that.

"Randolph, so glad to have you with us today," said Rev. Pillsbury, handing him a chocolate watermelon Sunday with sprinkles. Welcoming as always.

"Thank you, Pastor. You got a minute for me to ask you a religious question?"

"I always have time for a religious question," he assured the disfigured man. It was difficult to look him in the eye, with three to choose from.

"Are angels real?"

"Well, I like to think so. It's a matter of faith, I suppose."

"So when someone dies he becomes an angel?"

The pastor gave that a moment of consideration, then gently replied, "We believe that at death a Christian's soul passes immediately into the presence of God ... and the unbeliever's soul is eternally separated from God unto condemnation."

"So I did see Fritz Berber's soul on the way to heaven," grinned Three Eyes. "I sure hope he was a Christian."

~ ~ ~

Immigrants from Scotland and Ireland brought Presbyterianism to America as early as 1640. In 1706, seven ministers established the first American presbytery at Philadelphia. The PCA has its roots in theological controversies over liberalism in Christianity versus neo-orthodoxy. Affiliating itself with the liberal side, First Presbyterian teaches that one should take modern knowledge, science, and ethics into consideration over blindly following doctrinal authority.

So, the question of angels was a tricky one.

No one could scientifically prove there was such a thing. Or prove there wasn't.

Rev. Pillsbury was a widower, but he'd met a number of nice women in his congregation. Word was he was "seeing" Cindy Yager. She worked at her mother's shop, The Clothes Horse Boutique on South Main. A pretty woman in her mid 30s, she was a former Miss Watermelon Days Queen just like her mom.

Phillip Pillsbury was a big Clint Eastwood fan, giving him the inspiration for the church's Spaghetti Western night. Cindy Yager helped cook the big pot of spaghetti or linguini for each screening. $5 included both movie and pasta, a nice contribution to the church's youth fund. Nobody objected to the blazing six-guns in *A Fistful of Dollars* or *For a Few Dollars More*, but he doubted he could get away with a Dirty Harry Dinner.

Birdie Longstreet was a member of the First Presbyterian congregation. Rev. Pillsbury hoped his permissive attitude toward all those Spaghetti Westerns had not contributed to the old woman's nonchalance in shooting Fritz Berber stone-cold dead. Clint Eastwood had nothing on Miss Birdie when it came to "*Go ahead, make my day*" sentiments. Word was, she'd hit the mailman square between the eyes. Pretty good shooting, one had to admit.

Rev. Pillsbury made a note to include Miss Birdie in his prayers tonight.

# CHAPTER NINETEEN

## The Crashed Space Ship

Surprisingly, Birdie Longstreet wasn't particularly upset over the shooting incidence with Fritz Berber. To her dizzy state of mind, it seemed more like something she'd seen on TV than a real-life event.

She was more concerned about that Spaceman she had seen in her yard. Did that mean there had been another Moon Landing? Had the returning rocket ship – what did they call it, *The Challenger*? – crashed somewhere near town and that Spaceman was Buzz Lightyear wandering around lost, not sure how to get back to NASA?

Houston, do we have a problem?

Maybe she should report the sighting to the police, she told herself. Wasn't that what a good citizen would do? She picked up her phone and dialed 9-1-1. She had memorized the number. Or was that the date of that bombing at the World Trade Center in New York? She sometimes got numbers confused, she reminded herself.

"Po-lice Department," came the dispatcher's creamy voice. "How may I assist you?" Elvina was on duty this afternoon; her sister Myrtle was off to the animal shelter to acquire a dog for them. A burglar deterrent.

"This is Beatrice Longstreet. I want to report a wrecked space shuttle, *The Challenger*."

95

"Hello, Miss Birdie," sighed Elvina. "Where is this crash?" Probably the Bjorn kids shooting off bottle rockets, she figured. Leftover fireworks from the Fourth of July.

"Somewhere outside of town. Tell one of your deputies to give Buzz Aldrin a ride back to the NASA headquarters in Houston, Texas. He seemed a little lost when I saw him."

"Sure thing, Miss Birdie." She carefully disconnected the line. Turning back to her crossword puzzle, she didn't even bother writing up a police report. With Birdie Longstreet's history of false alarms, it wasn't necessary Chief Teague had told her.

~ ~ ~

"Hey, Babs," shouted Three Eyes to get his sister's attention. "Do you still work for McGuffey's Cabinet of Curiosities?"

"Who wants to know?"

"Me, Randolph – I'm the one asking you. Can't you see that? I'm standing right here."

"Oh, I thought it might've been Rex."

His sister was one of the few people who knew that he and his vanishing twin sometimes switched roles, Rex controlling the body instead of him. It was a good way to get some rest, snoozing inside, turning over the physical actions to his brother. That way, their shared entity could keep going nearly 24 hours a day without apparent sleep. Rex tended to be a night owl.

"About that freak show where you work –?"

"Yes, I still work for McGuffey's. Pay's good. And I like to travel." Contrary to most impressions, microcephalic people are not necessarily mentally diminished. Babs had a degree in socioeconomics, but she preferred a carney's life on the road.

"I thought I saw the McGuffey truck parked in town, that's all."

"Yes, that's what I'm doing home for the weekend. We had a layover between shows, so Professor McGuffey stopped over to visit his favorite nephew. The boy and his wife just moved here, he said."

"Is his nephew the new director at the retirement home up on the hill?"

"That's him, Benjamin Nelson. Married to an Indian lady. An India Indian, not a squaw-type Indian."

"Yeah, I know her. She's got three eyes like me."

"She might have a dot in the middle of her forehead, but there's nobody like you, Brother Dear."

# CHAPTER TWENTY

## Shiva the Destroyer

**B**ig Ed Crackleton was a local crime lord who managed a crew (mostly relatives) of young boys and girls who burgled houses, snatched purses, and picked pockets. No armed robberies or heavy-handed thuggery. Just grab-and-run stuff.

He had a good fence over in Burpyville (his cousin Big Nose Barney) who paid him top dollar for TV sets, jewelry, watches, and credit cards. The proceeds were distributed equally among the family – that is to say, members of the Crackleton clan who resided there at the Crossing.

Big Ed was second in command, with the family ruled by the iron hand of his sister Cecilia – better known as that crazy Granny Crackleton. She must be over 100 years old and thoroughly demented. Ed didn't pay much mind to her orders these days. In most cases, the old witch woman had forgotten her commands within fifteen minutes of issuing them.

Granny Crackleton wasn't really a witch, although with her tangled hair and dried-prune features certainly looked like one. Kids were afraid to walk past her shack on Halloween or dark moonless nights.

Big Ed's son Jeb was the local loan shark. He shared his take with the family too, although everybody knew he skimmed money off the top. He did business at a table in the back corner of the local convenience store, a row of hardback chairs forming a waiting area for Jeb's clients. Mostly, Jeb's borrowers were dirt-poor farmers and residents of Melon Hill, the lower-class section of town that backed up to the Pleasant Grove Cemetery.

Lydia Lazynski was into Jeb for $600, an amount she had no way of repaying – unless her well-to-do daughter coughed up an unlikely gift. Holly Eberhart Pfizer was not known to be generous, leaving her mother all-but-abandoned there in that rathole known as Melon Hill.

As a former state quilting champion, Holly was a minor celebrity who hobnobbed with the governor and high-level politicians. She was popular at crafts conventions and state fairs. She had written a new book that was getting good reviews.

The only asset Lydia Lazynski had that interested Jeb was a patchwork quilt sewn by Lydia's daughter, the very quilt that won her that first state championship. It was valued at $10,000. Jeb's fence would pay two grand for it.

Jeb had hoped to get it as settlement of Lydia's debt, but the old biddy had somehow been keeping up with her ever-increasing loan payments. He was getting impatient.

Jeb called on his dad for a little – what was that Latin phrase? – *Deus Ex Machina*. Help from God. Well, actually help from Big Ed's minions. Forget about waiting for Lydia to default on her loan. Why not send a kid in a side window to filch the prize quilt from its place on the wall of Lydia's cramped living room.

Big Ed agreed to the plan, assuming he got half the fence's payment.

# CHAPTER TWENTY-ONE

## Mickey Mouse

Mickey Crackleton was one of Big Ed's best burglars. At only twelve years old, he had pulled off a major robbery at the local Home Depot last year, making off with eight riding lawnmowers. He drove each one out of a hole in the storage yard's chain-link fence all by himself, delivering them to a waiting truck.

Mickey was one of the many illegitimate sons of Faith Ann, Jeb's sister. That also made him Deputy Gus Bentley's brother (or more likely half-brother). His mom ran the convenience store where Jeb conducted his loan-shark business. Despite being a Crackleton, Faith Ann had no known deformities. Nor did Mickey.

Unless larceny was genetic.

~ ~ ~

Mickey slithered through the cracked window with the agility of a ferret. Having no air conditioning, Lydia Lazynski left her windows open during the summer months, hoping to catch a breeze. The boy tumbled inside without so much as rustling the curtains.

The quilt was hanging right there on the living room wall where Three Eyes had said it would be. His cousin had almost got himself arrested scouting out the place. Mickey had to stand on an end table to dislodge the quilt from its hooks.

The design was called a Double Diamond, a variation that had earned Lydia's daughter the state championship many years ago. One reviewer said, "The delicate needlework combined with the dramatic angles make this a patchwork quilt for the ages." Another wrote, "Colorful, inventive, a new twist on an old theme." It was the quilt that had launched Holly Eberhart's career.

Holly's reputation had been flagging since being replaced as state quilting champion by Lizzie Ridenour. But her new book – *The History of Quiltmaking in Indiana* – was something of a comeback. This surge of popularity had increased the value of her quilts. This first prizewinner had seen a spike in value, jumping from $8,000 to $10,000. That was the opinion of The National Association of Certified Quilt Judges.

NACQJ was established in October 2015 to represent a group of judges certified by the former National Quilting Association. They hail from California to Rhode Island, from Texas to Minnesota; and are qualified to evaluate quilts and quiltmakers.

These Certified Judges had designated this as a Masterpiece Quilt, an "outstanding example of consummate skill in design, workmanship, and quilting."

To Big Ed, this Masterpiece rating simply meant the quilt was worth stealing. And Mickey was just the boy for the job.

Because of his quiet-as-a-mouse stealthiness, his buddies called him Mickey Mouse. He once broke into the safe at Food Lion in the middle of the day, the store filled with shoppers, without anyone hearing a thing. That take had been $417.37, a pretty good haul.

Pickings were slim around these parts.

He rolled up the Holly Eberhard Double Diamond quilt and tied it with twine but didn't make off with the prize for just then he'd heard Lydia Lazynski fumbling with her keys at the front door. Dropping everything, he raced into the kitchen and tugged at the back door – but it was locked.

"Hey, who's in there," shouted the Lazynski woman, catching a flash of movement from the corner of her eye as she opened the door. The rolled-up quilt on the floor was a clue that she had an intruder.

"Gotcha," she yelled as she slammed the kitchen door shut and locked it. Then, reaching for her phone, she dialed 9-1-1 to report a burglary in progress.

~ ~ ~

Addy Nelson enjoyed exploring her new neighborhood. Caruthers Corners was a small town, not much ground to cover. The twin hillocks overlooking the town – sites of the Perricock Museum of Science & History and the new retirement home where her husband worked – offered reference points that usually kept her from getting lost. But today she had gotten turned around and wandered into that glum section known as Melon Hill, a few square blocks behind the cemetery that sorely awaited gentrification.

Here, the houses were shabbier, in need of paint, missing shingles from the roofs, yards scattered with debris ranging from abandoned sofas to tireless cars on blocks. Mayor Tidemore's Beautification Program had hit fallow ground when it reached Melon Hills. New regulations and legal citations had not done the trick. People in this neighborhood were just too poor to keep up their houses. Fines rarely got paid by the scofflaws who defiantly lived here.

Addy was a little uncomfortable in this area of dilapidation and squalor, although statistics showed the crime rate to be de minimis. Mostly petty burglaries and purse snatching. But she saw no one on the street to snatch her Kate Spade shoulder bag. Just let them try. She carried a vial of pepper spray in her left hand – at the ready.

She was taken aback when she saw a movement out of the corner of her eye. That house over there, angled in a way that she could see into its backyard. What was that dark blur that came tumbling out of the doggie door and scampered into the shed in the far corner of the yard. The shed door was cracked just enough to allow entry.

Oh my, she thought. Somebody's pet on the run. If she moved quickly, she could trap it in the shed where it had taken temporary refuge.

Always the good citizen – she was now a naturalized American – Addy stepped through the rickety gate, crossed the bare-dirt yard and slammed the shed door closed, flipping the hatch lock into place, securing the wayward animal.

Pulling out her iPhone, she was about to call the animal rescue number at Strays & Others but hesitated when a police cruiser stopped outside the gate. Tommy Truehart stepped outside the car, his service revolver drawn, a two-hand grip.

"Stop where you are!" he shouted. "Raise your hand to where I can see 'em."

Addy Nelson complied, her heart quickening its beat. "What's the problem, officer?"

"Had a report of a burglary in process and you're the only one I see trespassing on Mrs. Lazynski's premises."

"I was just helping catch a stray dog."

"Dog, what dog?"

"I've got it locked up in the shed here."

"Best we call animal control for that," he said.

"I was just about to do that."

At that moment, the back door flew open to reveal Lydia Lazynski looking all aflutter. "Did you get him?' she shouted to the policeman. "He escaped through the dog door."

"Your dog?" said the deputy."

"I don't have a dog."

"You've got a dog door."

"That was already here when I bought this house. Old Mrs. Pruett had a Pekingese. I'm talking about a real human-being intruder. One of Big Ed Crackleton's boys, I'd guess. A wiry little bugger, he was. The boy was trying to steal Holly's prizewinning quilt. I'm Holly Eberhard's mom, y' know."

"Yessum, I know," nodded Tommy Truehart. "I've lived here all my life."

"Of course, you have. I know your mother. She's a fine Christian woman."

Tommy nodded his acknowledgement. He wasn't very religious himself, but his mother attended church every Sunday. "Let's have a look at who or what this young lady has trapped in your shed.

She spoke up. "My name's Addy Nelson. My husband is the new director of the retirement center."

The deputy nodded. "I've met him. People speak well of your husband. Say he's doing a great job up there with all them old-timers." He pointed his Smith & Wesson at the shed door. "Now if you and Mrs. Lazynski will step back, I'm gonna open this door."

The two women retreated to the edge of the fenced-in yard, careful not to trip over the old tires and other junk.

Tommy undid the latch and eased the door open. "Whoever's in there better come out peacefully. I have a gun and I'm prepared to use it if need be."

"Don't shoot," came a high-pitched voice. "I'm coming out with my hands up."

~ ~ ~

"So, you're Mickey Mouse," said Police Chief Harry Teague. He and the boy were sitting in the tiny interrogation room at the police station. The walls were painted gray. There was a small squarish window in center of the metal door. The only furnishings were a scarred metal table and four chairs. The table was bolted to the cement floor.

"That's what they call me, but I'm a Crackleton and proud of it."

"We've heard of you – Big Ed's top cat burglar. But this time you came out through a dog door, I'm told."

"I got cornered in the kitchen. That old bag came home too soon."

"You're not denying it?"

"Why bother? Your deputy caught me dead to rights. But I'm not worried. I'm only twelve – underage for jail time in this state."

"True, but we've got some good reform schools for minors. Might be just the place for you, young man."

"Go ahead. I'll run away. Or Big Ed will bust me out."

"Don't be so sure about that."

"Says you."

"I'm the police chief, so I'm the one who says."

# CHAPTER TWENTY-TWO

## McGuffey's Cabinet of Curiousities

**P**rofessor Peter Baines McGuffey ("Professor" was a self-bestowed honorific) was enjoying his visit with his nephew Benny. The boy had done well for himself. A good job with that retirement center. A fine wife. Now if he would just produce a few offspring ....

McGuffey didn't have any children of his own. Benny's kids would be as close to grandchildren as he would ever come. He was thinking about selling the traveling roadshow and settling down in Caruthers Corners to be near his nephew. He was already past retirement age.

He knew the area well. Several of his sideshow performers came from nearby Crackleton Crossing. It was a great repository for freaks, human oddities, and fascinating deformities. Chalk it up to mankind's innate curiosity that audiences would pay good money to view "nature's mistakes."

In his show this season, he had a pinhead (Babs Johnson), a lobster boy (one of Phil Jinks's kids), two midgets (a guy from Cincinnati and his wife), a man with three arms (he'd come over from Applerouth's Oddities & Rides for a bump in pay), the Wild Girl from Borneo (a pretty good actress), a firebreather, a geek who bit the heads off chickens, and a two-headed calf. McGuffey's Cabinet of Curiosities provided the sideshow attraction for traveling circuses. He had a pretty decent working relationship with Barley's Big Top.

At 75, Pete McGuffey was still a vigorous man with a thick shock of gray hair and a prominent potbelly, but he looked pretty official (in a Willy Wonka kind of way) in his top hat and tails. He acted as the show's barker.

The truck parked in front of Benjamin Nelson's two-story Victorian house hauled the tents and poles and pulleys that provided a home for the sideshow. The performers and roustabouts followed in three vans. One of the vans pulled a trailer holding the two-headed calf and a crate of chickens. The little caravan prowled the backroads of Indiana, Illinois, and Ohio – sometimes going as far south as Missouri or as far west as Iowa and Nebraska.

Touring provided a decent living for the little troupe. But freak shows were a dying business. Staring at people with deformities had become unPC in today's Woke World. Too bad. These people depended on him for their livelihood.

~ ~ ~

"Let's do it," said Maddy Madison. "Aggie and N'yen are all grown up. I miss having young kids around the house."

"You're just looking for somebody to bake watermelon cookies for," chuckled her husband. "You bake them faster than I can eat 'em."

Maddy appraised her husband's lanky frame. "You don't seem to be putting on any weight."

"I get lots of exercise."

"How? Sitting in that boat all day with Edgar?"

"Loading that boat in and out of the water is strenuous."

"Okay, whatever you say. But what about that kid Chief Teague is holding down there in that cell?"

"Mickey Crackleton ...."

"Mickey Mouse, they call him. And he's as cute as a little mouse."

"So, how long would he be living here with us?"

"Maybe a week, two at the most. We'd just be fostering him until his hearing. Then he'd be put into the children's services system or packed off to a reformatory."

"I'd hate to see that," muttered Beau.

"Me too. He *is* one of my kin, after all – a Crackleton."

"Don't remind me. I'd hate to think you might turn into a Granny Crackleton in your senior years."

"Don't worry. I won't look like that scraggly-haired old loon as long as the Helen of Troy Spa and Beauty Saloon remains open for business."

"That's reassuring."

"So, what do you say, Hon? Judge Cramer says he'll approve our fostering the boy if we give him the word."

"Oh, let's do it," sighed Beau. "I've missed kids around the place too. Maybe I can teach him how to fish."

# CHAPTER TWENTY-THREE

## The Business Proposition

**W**hile Professor Pete McGuffey was in town, he hoped to recruit a headliner for his Cabinet of Curiosities. Babs Johnson had a brother with three eyes. Now that would be a terrific draw. She'd promised to talk to him about joining her on the road.

Getting good help was challenging.

Conjoined twins were hard to come by. They occur once in every 60,000 births. Approximately 70 percent of conjoined twins are female; most are stillborn.

Vanishing twins were a different story. They occur in one of every eight multifetus pregnancies. However, in many cases they may not even be known. One twin absorbs the other in the womb before anybody notices the duality.

The rate of twins among live births is only about 1.3% But as many as 12% of all naturally conceived pregnancies may *begin* as twin pregnancies.

Approximately 7% to 36% of IVF pregnancies involving multiples are diagnosed with Vanishing Twins Syndrome. Research suggests that VTS is more common among pregnant people over 30.

People with four legs or an extra arm were a dime a dozen, but finding someone with two heads or three eyes was hard to come by.

Technically, Parasitic Twins are not the same as Conjoined Twins. Conjoined Twins are two fully developed fetuses that are connected at birth. They share one or more organs and are usually attached at their back, chest or torso. A Parasitic Twin is the combination one fully developed fetus and one undeveloped fetus. The undeveloped fetus is nonfunctional and doesn't survive the pregnancy. He or she may not be visible at all. Or else the only evidence of the presence might be a stray hand sticking out of a stomach or an extra leg.

Some medical experts classified Randolph Johnson as a Parasitic Twin. With the Vanishing Twin Syndrome, an ultrasound shows two fetuses in early pregnancy. Later on, only one fetus remains. With a Parasitic Twin, one of the twins doesn't totally absorb, leaving parts of its body attached to the dominant twin.

Randolph and his brother Rex didn't draw distinctions. They were who they were. They were comfortable with being called freaks. BFD, they said.

~ ~ ~

McGuffey was prepared to pay top dollar for Randolph Johnson.

He was pretty sure Babs would talk her brother into joining the troupe. She got lonely. Not many people wanted to hang out with a pinhead.

Microcephaly is a condition where a baby's head is much smaller than expected. During pregnancy, a baby's head grows because the baby's brain grows. Microcephaly can occur because a baby's brain has not developed properly during pregnancy or has stopped growing after birth, which results in a smaller head size.

Many babies born with microcephaly may demonstrate no other symptoms at birth but go on to develop epilepsy, cerebral palsy, learning disabilities, hearing loss, and vision problems. In some rare cases, children with microcephaly develop entirely normal except for the shape of their head.

Babs was one of the lucky ones. Her intellectual facilities were perfectly intact, but she looked like something out of Tod Browning's once-banned movie *Freaks* – pointed head and all.

Elvira Snow and her sister Jenny Lee had been featured in Tod Browning's 1932 horror flick. In real life, they had performed on the sideshow circuit as Pip and Flip.

Another pinhead, Schlitzie Surtees appeared in that movie also. His lifelong career on the outdoor entertainment circuit with shows like Barnum & Bailey made him into a cultural icon of the times.

Perhaps the most famous was Zip the Pinhead (William Henry Johnson). When P.T. Barnum recruited Zip in 1860, he shaved his head except for a tuft of hair at the top, giving rise to the pinhead description. Zip outlasted Barnum's solo ventures, going on to work with Ringling Bros. and Barnum and Bailey, at the Coney Island pavilions, and in dime museums across the US of A.

Babs Johnson wasn't so well known. What with the shrinking market for sideshows, she didn't get seen by as many people. She was thinking of building a website and launching a weekly podcast. Babs was disappointed to find that someone had already claimed the domain name – Freakshow.com.

# CHAPTER TWENTY-FOUR

## The Walls have Ears

**"Y**ou've gotta let it go," Beau Madison said to his wife over the dinner table that night. "I'm sorry that I ever told you about Bobby Ray Purdue burying something under that tree in his backyard."

"I can't help myself," sighed Maddy, serving another fried pork tenderloin to Mickey. Ever since they started fostering the boy, he had been eating like a horse. Well, at least like a small pony. "My curiosity is driving me crazy," she added with a roll of her eyes. "Something odd is going on there."

Beau shook his head. "You know what they said about the cat ..."

"Yes, yes, I know. The girls suggested I ought to go dig it up if I was so darned curious."

"You'd never get away with that," cautioned her husband. "Bobby Ray has that place surrounded by security cameras and goodness knows what all. He may even have machinegun terrets. He installed all kind of deterrents after that break-in a few years ago. Nobody could get near his house."

"I could."

Maddy and Beau turned their attention to Mickey Mouse. "What?" they said in unison.

"I could break in. I've done it before."

"Y-you have?" stammered Maddy.

"Yes'um. Big Ed had me do it. I am – uh, was – the best burglar he's got. Last time I did it, I made off with a bag of rare Morgan silver dollars. Worth a small fortune. Big Ed was right happy with me."

Beau's eyebrows were raised in alarm, like two caterpillars rearing up to do battle on his forehead. "You were a thief?"

"You know that. It's why I'm here under house arrest. I got caught trying to filch that old lady's patchwork quilt. Big Ed said it was rightfully his, that she owed him money."

"You're not under house arrest," Maddy said defensively. "We're merely fostering you till your court date."

"I'm not worried about going to court."

"Why not?"

"'Cause I'm under age. They can't do nothing to me till I turn eighteen. I'm only twelve. Big Ed says I got a great criminal career ahead of me ... at least for six more years. Then I'll go into management, running a crew of my own."

"That's the way it works, huh?" said Beau, barely able to hide the astonishment in his voice.

"You bet. Haven't you noticed that most of us Crackletons don't have no jobs. A used car lot and a convenience store are about the only businesses at the Crossing. Stealing is the family's main business. Profits are divided amongst the whole tribe, so nobody but the procurers – thieves, to you – has to work."

"Jeb Crackleton runs a loan shark business, I hear."

"Uncle Jeb is an exception. He's what you call an entrepreneur. Does things on his own."

"Well, you're going to have to change your ways," scolded Maddy. "Or else you'll end up in a reform school."

"That don't seem fair," Mickey grunted, then turned back to his uneaten pork tenderloin. "Stealing is h family business."

~ ~ ~

Three Eyes was what Big Ed called a "scout." Mickey Mouse was a "procurer." And Big Nose Barney, over in Burpyville, was a "converter," i.e. a fence who converted stolen goods into cash.

Big Nose Barney had an oversized proboscis, a nose with the proportions of a rutabaga. He went by the surname of Brown, but this deformity was proof that he was a Crackleton by birth. He ran a "front" company, Barney Brown's Bail & Pawn. According to his last inventory, half the goods in the pawn shop were stolen.

Dumpster diving was a good excuse for Three Eyes to be poking around neighborhoods, keeping his eyes (all three) open for opportunities. Sometimes it was spotting an easy entry like an open window. Other times it was noting valuables like TV sets or jewelry or Lydia Lazynski's rare patchwork quilt. Sometimes it was picking up information that so-and-so was going to be out of town – on vacation or visiting a relative or something like that – leaving their home unguarded.

Big Ed was a clever businessman. Not only did he own the pawnshop that sold his ill-gotten items, but he also owned Silver Bells Security, a company that installed most of the home security systems around here. Out of necessity, he was a silent partner.

Silver Bells had installed the security system for Bobby Ray Purdue's ultra-modern house out there in the middle of a watermelon field. For Mickey, it was like having a key to the front door.

~ ~ ~

Police Chief Harry Teague didn't like to admit to the growing number of burglaries in his town. He poo-pooed the suggestion that break-ins were on the rise. He cited statistics (carefully chosen) to show that B&Es were not a major civic concern.

However, truth be known, burglaries were a big problem. He knew Big Ed Crackleton was the man behind them. But it was hard to make any charges stick with Big Ed's crews of underage thieves.

When things got too hot, Big Ed would simply shift his operations to adjacent towns. It kept the police chasing their tails.

The Caruthers Corners Police Department was small, not having enough manpower to quell the onslaught of professional criminals from Crackleton Crossing. The Town Council regularly turned down the police chief's request for more officers, having decided that the cost of extra men would exceed the losses. These were petty thefts they were dealing with, not major heists or bank robberies.

Chief Teague knew his mandate was not to totally extinguish crime, but rather to keep it down to a manageable level. Cutting off the snake's head was the best way to stop it. But Big Ed remained elusive, difficult to prosecute. His fingerprints were not found in any of the burglarized homes. He never left his easy chair. Or that table at the convenience store. His minions took care of most everything. Big Nose Barney handled the rest.

~ ~ ~

As it happened, a few years ago Jeb Crackleton got sent to prison for a spell, as did his wayward sons El and Vis, but before you could say *snap!* Jeb was back at his popular loansharking business.

That early release had cost him a bundle. Since then, he'd been very careful to avoid any run-ins with the law.

When people asked Jeb about his line of work, he simply said, "Banking."

# CHAPTER TWENTY-FIVE

## The New Guy

Aggie met Bobby Elwood for lunch on Monday. Cozy Café was having a daily special, Pork Tenderloin platters with cole slaw and hushpuppies. Hoosiers would not be who they are without their regular diet of fried pork tenderloin.

Bobby came from work, still wearing his coveralls with *Elwood's Bug Busters* emblazoned on the back. On his left breast pocket, it simply said *Bobby*. He smelled of bug spray. Fortunately, Cozy Café wasn't a fancy place. Nonetheless, Maisie seated them at a far table, "downwind from other eaters," she winked.

"Busy morning," Bobby halfway apologized. "We're tenting Ed Kensinger's house. I left my new guy in charge while I'm meeting you for lunch. He's working out just fine."

"Who is your new guy? Do I know him?"

"Not likely. He came over from Fort Wayne recently. Had good references from the Orkin franchise there."

"You'll have to introduce me. What's his name."

"Mikey – Mikey Slovak. Polish or Czech I think."

"Does he have a family?"

"No, a single guy. He seems to like it that way. Pretty much keeps to himself. Has an apartment over at Madison Arms."

"Who's helping with the tenting." She knew Bobby hired local guys when he needed help with a job.

"David and Zeke Wagler. Them Amish are hard workers – whether you're building a barn or tenting a house. Not afraid of heights either." Bobby Elwood had a touch of acrophobia. Anything higher than a stepladder gave him vertigo. That was a drawback when tenting a house. Many of the structures around here tended to be three stories.

"Desert?" asked Maisie, showing up at their table precisely as they finished off the tenderloin platters. Maisie Walters might be one of the wealthiest people in town, but she still worked a daily shift in her diner. She liked cooking and she liked the social interplay with her neighbors.

"Do you have watermelon shortcake today?" asked Aggie.

"You bet, Hon."

"That's for me."

"Me too," echoed Bobby. "But I'll have to eat and run. I've gotta get back to work."

~ ~ ~

Sissy often packed her own lunch, eating it in the coffee kiosk corner of the library. Today was a peanut butter and pickle sandwich on Wonder bread. Her eating habits would turn a nutritionist's tummy.

The thick Baltimore Geographical Society study was still on the book cart to be replaced on its proper shelf, so she lugged the tome over to her table to thumb through it out of curiosity. She'd never read the whole thing, a technical treatise on consanguinity and eugenics.

Scanning the yellowed pages, she was surprised to see some names she recognized, people who were still resident in nearby Crackleton Crossing three decades after the study had been conducted. There was Sarah Celine Crackleton – better known as Granny – matriarch of the close-knit clan. And Granny's brother Ed. And Four-Footed Freddy. And Skinny Minnie. And Legless Larry.

On page 273, she found a photograph of Big Ed's son Jebediah, all 6-foot-10 of him, along with his dwarf son Willard – better known as Dub. And on the facing page was a photo of Randolph, his three eyes staring back at the camera. Standing next to him was his sister Babs, her pinhead shaved bare except for a fuzzy topnotch.

Sissy had to admit she was a bit shocked by the pictures. She saw all these people around town on a regular basis, not giving them another thought. But to view them inside this book, like mug shots on a post office wall, was unsettling. It made her realize these neighbors were afflicted with severe medical abnormalities, the product of reckless inbreeding and genetic aberrations.

Those cuckoo Crackletons!

The one she knew best was Gus Bentley, Aunt Cookie's adopted son. She'd seen his webbed toes when they went swimming at Wagler's Pond. The boy had been born with six toes on each foot, an oddity, but not visible when he had his boots on. Now, he was a policeman, the newest addition to the force. Chief Teague said he was "working out just fine."

Gus – born Augustus Erasmus Crackleton, one of Faith Ann Crackleton's numerous illicit children – was too young to have been listed in the 1994 study. But Sissy counted eight of his brothers as she paged through the book. Two of them had extra pinkie fingers, one was said to have extra toes like Gus, and four suffered from hypertrichosis, a hirsute condition commonly known as Werewolf Syndrome. Her oldest son Louis seemed to be normal.

And there was Gutless Gary, born with his intestines on the outside of his body. And Lassie Larry, who had a canine-like face. And Bendable Burt, the human pretzel. And Crocodile Curtis, who had reptilian skin. And let's not overlook Backward Bartholomew, whose head was turned around facing where he was coming from – "better than having a rearview mirror," he often said. And Bird Boy, a guy who had a beak instead of lips.

Crackletons, all.

It was as if God had put their genes into a Veg-O-Matic and turned it on full blast.

Oh my.

All of a sudden, she felt queasy. Had the pictures in this study upset her that much?

Sissy closed the book and pushed her sandwich aside, having lost her appetite.

# CHAPTER TWENTY-SIX

## Look What the Mouse Dragged In

"Got it," Mickey Mouse announced over breakfast. Maddy was serving up watermelon pancakes with homemade whipped cream. Add a little powdered sugar, they were delish.

"Got what, dear?" she said absently, careful not to burn the pancakes on the electric griddle. The temperature dial was a little off.

"That box you wanted, the one Bobby Ray buried."

"What?" She looked up from the hissing griddle, a puzzled look on her face.

"A box, you say," Beau spoke up, his attention turning from his stack of pancakes to the boy.

"Right," nodded Mickey. "That one you saw Bobby Ray bury under the willow tree behind his house."

"What about it?"

"I dug it up last night. That's it over there on the corner table." He pointed to a rusty toolbox.

Maddy looked confused. "Why did you do that?"

"You said you wanted it, didn't you?"

"Yes, but –"

"You both been good to me, letting me stay here with you instead of letting me rot in jail. I wanted to do something to thank you."

"But how did you get past all the security?" asked Beau.

"Told you, I been out there before. I know the security code to turn off the alarms and cameras and lasers and stuff."

"How did you get the code?"

"Trade secret," he grinned, careful not to mention Silver Bells Security. That was a no-no.

"What's in the box?' asked Maddy, unable to contain her curiosity.

"Dunno. I haven't opened it. Thought that honor belonged to you, Mrs. Madison."

"Beau?"

"Go ahead," he sighed. "May as well see what we stole."

Maddy turned off the griddle and removed the last pancakes, then made her way to the corner table. "Here goes," she said, grasping the clasps.

The rectangular container was constructed of metal, an old toolbox judging by the word CRAFTSMAN stamped onto the side. It was rusty from having been buried in the damp ground. The nearby river keeps the soil moist. The hinges squeaked like tiny rodents when Maddy pried the box open.

"Oh my," she said when she looked inside. "This cannot be right."

There in the box was a pistol.

~ ~ ~

There was no law against Bobby Ray Purdue owning a pistol. Indiana is a permitless carry state, meaning that Indiana residents can carry a gun without a license. To be eligible to purchase a gun in Indiana, you must be at least 18 years old and meet certain other requirements, such as:

• Not having been convicted of a crime that carries a sentence of more than one year

- Not having been convicted of domestic violence
- Not having a history of alcohol or drug abuse
- Not having a history of violence or emotional instability
- Not having a history of involuntary commitment
- Not having been adjudicated as mentally incompetent

Check, check, and check. Bobby Ray was eligible on all counts.

The mysterious thing was why would he be burying a pistol. Was he hiding evidence of some unknown crime?

~ ~ ~

"Don't touch it," advised Beau, leaning over his wife's shoulder to look inside the metal box. "You don't want your fingerprints on it."

"True," Maddy nodded. "Nobody buries a pistol unless it's been involved in something bad."

"Like a murder?" squeaked Mickey, his eyes wide. He looked scared. "Do you think he killed somebody?"

"Could be just a robbery," said Beau in an attempt to calm the boy.

"Bobby Ray is filthy rich," Maddy pointed out. "He doesn't need to rob anybody – at least, not with a pistol."

"And if he wanted someone dead, he'd hire it done," added Beau snarkily.

"Bobby Ray is not a violent man," argued Maddy. "He's more like a little boy who never grew up."

"You mean like Peter Pan?" said Mickey.

"Yes, like that."

"We need to report this to Chief Teague," declared Beau. Law-abiding to the core.

"No so fast," cautioned his wife. "We didn't come to finding this suspicious gun in an entirely legal way." She eyed the boy sitting across the table, scarfing down pancakes like there was no tomorrow. He was small for his age, but ate like he was trying to catch up.

Beau nodded slowly. "Yes, I see what you mean – Mickey's midnight excursion."

"Maybe you could just poke around a little," suggested Maddy. "See what you can find out from Harry Teague before you spill the beans on our little friend's extracurricular activities."

"Extracurricular?" said Mickey with a mouthful of pancakes. "I ain't in school. I'm being – whatcha call it? – homeschooled."

"Homeschooled to be a thief," muttered Beau. No longer interested in his breakfast.

"Now, now, let's not be judgmental," said Maddy. "Mickey was under the influence of Ed Crackleton, a most detestable individual."

Beau leaned closer to examine the gun. "That's a British Enfield No. 2 Mk 1," he observed. "A 38-caliber model. See, it's stamped right there on the barrel. A top-break pistol, the Enfield No. 2 shoots Smith & Wesson 200 grain LRN's. It's the only service revolver that uses that ammunition. Should be easy to trace to any crimes by the ballistics." A Vietnam vet, he knew his guns. Even better than his outdoorsy pal Edgar Ridenour.

Maddy slammed the metal lid shut. "I'm going to lock this box away in the safe under the stairs."

"You've got a safe?" asked Mickey Mouse.

"Don't get any ideas, young man," said Maddy. "You're in enough hot water as it is."

# CHAPTER TWENTY-SEVEN

## Silver Bells Security

**A**gnes Millicent Tidemore stopped by to deliver gifts for her sisters. They were teenagers now and had little interest in their now-grown-up older sister. No one was home but her mom.

"Today is National Secondhand Wardrobe Day," announced Aggie. "So, I'm passing these dresses along to the Terrible Trio." That was her nickname for her siblings.

"Today?" repeated Tilly Tidemore, Aggie's mother.

"August 25th," Aggie nodded. "Look it up."

"I guess there's a day for everything, isn't there?"

"Apparently. Tomorrow is International Read a Comic in Public Day. And the one after that is International Day Against Nuclear Tests."

"Oh my. That's quite a swing."

Aggie smiled. "I'm surprised nobody in Caruthers Corners celebrated August 3rd."

"Oh, what was that?"

"National Watermelon Day. After all, watermelons are a big deal around here, the county's largest crop."

Tilly shrugged. "We have the Watermelon Days Festival each year. I think that overshades August 3rd."

"Apparently so. Where shall I put these dresses?"

"Just toss them over that chair. I'll sort them out with your sisters when they get home. I think they are up at Haney's Petting Zoo. Your Uncle Freddie is doing one of his Sparkplug the Clown performances." Although Frederic Hollingsworth Madison was the town's fire chief, he enjoyed exhibiting his clown persona, a chance to hide his massive burn scars under a layer of colorful greasepaint.

"How are you doing?" asked Aggie carefully. Having grown up with a mother who lived in a fantasy world, she was cautious about the thin line of mental stability. Hypnotherapy had "cured" her mom, but Aggie worried that it might not be permanent.

"Me? I'm perfectly fine. Haven't seen any unicorns or fairies in years."

"Ah, that's good."

Tilly skillfully changed the topic. "I was over at your Grammy's earlier today. She and your Grampy are really enjoying fostering that that Crackleton boy. I think they miss you and N'yen being underfoot."

"Mickey Mouse? He will only be there for another week or so. His court date is coming up. He'll likely get sent to a correctional institution for adolescent boys – probably Indiana Boys School."

"Oh, that's too bad. I think Beau and Maddy would be heartbroken."

~ ~ ~

First thing N'yen did after the break-in was put new locks on his doors and install a security system. His friend Tommy Truehart installed security systems on the side, but wanting a professional job he called Silver Bells.

The guy who showed up was named Earl Kyle Brown, but the extra finger on his left hand indicated a Crackleton lineage. In an effort to be polite, N'yen didn't ask about it. Not everybody was proud of their heritage, he'd learned.

"Your house will be safe as Fort Knox," Earl Kyle Brown said in a practiced sales spiel. "Any intrusion will set off an alarm on your iPhone, be flagged on your computer, and set off a 120-decibel siren in both your bedroom and in your home office. At the same time, it will notify the local police department that you're experiencing a break-in and alert our office over in Burpyville. The police will immediately respond. And we will dispatch our adjusters to access any losses. You are covered by our blanket insurance policy, up to one million dollars. All this for a modest monthly fee."

The fee wasn't modest. But N'yen was willing to pay any price for his and his wife's safety.

~ ~ ~

On his way back to the Silver Bells Security headquarters in Burpyville, Earl Kyle Brown was humming that signature tune from Disney's *Snow White and the Seven Dwarfs* – "Whistle While You Work."

He felt he'd done a good sales job. That Asian guy – N'yen Madison, it said on the work order – had taken the upgrade, adding laser beams to his living room. Just like that scene in *Oceans 12*, that heist movie where Vincent Cassel dances through a laser grid in a secret room inside a mansion on the shores of Lake Como in Italy. Now that was a good movie.

Difference here, when Big Ed eventually decided to burglarize this house, there would be no need for his minions to avoid laser beams. All they needed was the code to turn off the security system. Easy peasy.

Earl Kyle Brown couldn't wait to get back to the office and tell his brother about the upgrade. Big Nose would be so proud of him.

# CHAPTER TWENTY-EIGHT

## Good to the Last Drop

Beau Madison was having a cup of black coffee at the Cozy Café when Police Chief Harry Teague walked in. Everybody in town knew Harry's habit of taking a midmorning coffee break. Maisie always had a cup waiting for him at the counter at precisely 10 a.m.

"Morning, Beau," said the police chief as he slid onto the stool next to the town's one-time mayor and former councilman. "How are the donuts today?" Harry had a sweet tooth.

"Not bad," the older man held up a half-eaten cinnamon with sprinkles as proof.

"Fresh out of the oven," said Maisie Walters as she sat a sturdy ceramic coffee mug in front of Chief Teague. Steam roiled out of it like from a locomotive's stack.

"Tastes more like a Cinnabon than a donut," added Beau.

"Then I'll take two," nodded Harry Teague. "I skipped breakfast this morning."

"You been busy?" Beau asked casually.

"The usual. Aside from the Fritz Berber murder, there was that business with Lydia Lazynsky – but you know about that, fostering the boy and all. Then there was that daylight burglary at your grandson's house. But I don't think that was connected to the Lazynsky robbery. Word is, Big Ed is riled that someone is working his territory. The Crackletons claim the town as their own."

"So I've heard." Back when Beau had been mayor, he and former police chief Jim Purdue had worked hard to keep Big Ed's larcenous activities in check. It was like playing Whac-A-Mole – catch one burglar or purse snatcher and up pops another!

"There was one other thing," said Harry Teague as he sank his incisors into the chewy cinnamon donut.

"Oh, what?" said Beau, his ears perking up.

"This is totally on the q.t. But somebody took a shot at N.L. Purdue, the bigwig over at the EZ Chair Seat Factory."

*Bingo!* thought Beau Madison.

~ ~ ~

Of course, revealing that someone had taken a shot at Newcombe Lamont Purdue in front of café-owner Maisie Walters was equivalent to blasting the news over a loudspeaker while driving down Main Street. But Beau didn't point that out to the police chief. He merely took another sip of coffee while muttering "Uh-huh."

"The assailant actually winged him," continued Harry. "But Doc Medford was able to patch the old boy up good as new."

"Who did it?"

"Don't know yet. N.L. isn't talking, but I'm pretty sure he recognized the shooter."

"Any suspects."

"Probably someone from the chair factory. A disgruntled employee. He does work 'em long and hard, pays 'em spit. Plus, there's been some layoffs lately. Economy's not been so good, y'know."

"True," nodded Beau. "My weekly groceries at Food Lion have been running $200 lately. And that's for just the two of us. Three, now that we have that foster kid."

"How's that working out?"

"Real good. He's fitting right in."

"Pleased to hear that," said the Police Chief. "Mickey's not a bad apple. Just need to get 'im out from under Big Ed's thumb. You can see how that worked out for Gus Bentley. He's one of the best deputies I've got."

"You only have four," Beau pointed out.

"Not counting the part-timers and crossing guards," Chief Teague said defensively. "But I could use more."

# CHAPTER TWENTY-NINE

## The Online Summit

**M**addy gathered her four best-est friends on another Zoom call. "Don't you see," she said after telling them about the pistol in the buried metal box, "Bobby Ray Purdue shot his brother. It's as plain as the nose on your face."

"Hey, no comments about my nose," grumbled Bootsie. Being 40 pounds overweight, she was sensitive about her appearance. Maddy herself was slightly rounded, but Lizzie and Cookie both were downright skinny. Or svelte, as they liked to say.

"Why would Bobby Ray try to kill his brother?" persisted Lizzie. "They're both rich. No inheritance to fight over."

"Sibling rivalry," suggested Bootsie. "Newcombe always lorded his wealth over other family members. Maybe Bobby Ray got fed up with his brother's bosting. I know Jim and I did."

"But Bobby Ray's even richer than N.L. these days," Cookie pointed out. With her super memory, she knew the financial statistics. She'd read them in *Forbes*.

"And N.L. resents that," answered Bootsie as if she had the inside track on Purdue family dynamics. "He can be very unforgiving."

"But Bobby Ray shot N.L. —not the other way around," stated Lizzie.

"The reason for their contretemps isn't important," said Maddy. "Question is, are we going to blow the whistle on Bobby Ray?"

"Absolutely," replied Bootsie.

"But he's your cousin," Cookie pointed out.

"Cousin or not, that's the right thing to do," insisted Bootsie. Having been a cop's wife most of her life, she was a law-and-order type through and through.

"And we've got the proof," said Maddy. "Ballistics will match that bullet Doc Medford took out of N.L.'s shoulder with the gun we found in the box. Case closed."

"Maybe not," countered Cookie. Her eidetic memory gave her impeccable logic. "All Bobby Ray has to do is deny that he buried that box."

"But Beau saw him do it."

"Bobby Ray's word against your hubby's – a standoff."

"But Beau is a direct descent from one of the town's Founding Fathers," huffed Maddy. "That oughta count for something."

"It does," said Cookie. "But Bobby Ray is rich, very rich. That counts for something too."

Lizzie jumped in. "Maybe they will find Bobby Ray's fingerprints on that toolbox."

"Doubtful," sighed Maddy. "The box is pretty rusted. And Mickey handled it when he brought it home. We don't want to tie him to how we came to have that pistol. He's on thin ice as is, his court date coming up soon."

"How about prints on the gun?" suggested Bootsie. Thinking like a cop's wife.

"Perhaps," allowed Maddy. "Nobody has touched the pistol. It's still in the box, just as we found it."

"You better be sure you have matching fingerprints before you go accusing Bobby Ray Purdue. Things could get nasty if you don't have any proof."

"How do we find that out?"

"I know," said Cookie. "I'll get Gus to dust the gun for fingerprints. He learned how to do that as part of his police training."

"Will he keep quiet about this until we know what we have?" asked Lizzie. Nervous about involving a police deputy.

Cookie sniffed defiantly. "Of course, he will if I ask him to. After all, I'm his mama – sorta."

# CHAPTER THIRTY

## Good Police Training

**B**obby Ray's fingerprints were still on file from when he'd turned up as a Lost Boy, one of the four kids who disappeared in Neverending Swamp back in 1984. After his years with the Haney Bros. Circus, he had changed a bit. Positive proof was needed to certify that he was the legitimate heir to Grandma Purdue's fortune – rare Grand Watermelon bills stashed inside a family patchwork quilt. The Quilters Club was credited with discovering the hidden money. And Bobby Ray had won out over his older brother.

"Yep, they're a match," nodded Chief Harry Teague when he compared the two cards. "You broke the case. How'd you do it."

"Aw, just good police work," replied Gus Bentley shyly.

"And how did you come up with the British Enfield No. 2?"

Gus licked his lips nervously. "My mother called me when the Quilters Club found the box."

"And how did they turn it up?"

That's when Maddy butted in, telling Chief Teague the story of her husband's fishing trip. "Beau saw it all. And he's willing to testify to that fact." Maddy, Lizzie, and Cookie had accompanied Gus to the meeting with the police chief.

"Yes, but how did you ladies get your hands on that buried toolbox?"

Maddy shrugged nonchalantly. "Dug it up. It appeared to have been abandoned."

"Hmm, that's a fine legal point," said Chief Teague.

"Do we need a lawyer?"

"Your son-in-law or your granddaughter?" he asked with a half-smirk.

"Take your pick."

"There could be a question of trespass," the Police Chief said.

"Not really," replied Cookie Bentley. "That willow tree is on my land. I still own the two hundred acres surrounding Bobby Ray's house."

"Good point," Chief Teague admitted.

"What now?" asked Maddy.

"Guess I'll take it from here," he sighed. "Next thing I need to do is have a chat with the man who donated a new police cruiser to the department last year."

"Tricky, isn't it," smiled Maddy.

"I hope he doesn't take the car back," said Harry Teague. "I like how it drives."

~ ~ ~

Maisie Walters closed Cozy Café early that afternoon to provide a neutral meeting place for the Purdue brothers and the Police Chief. Neither N.L. nor Bobby Ray wanted to be spotted going into the police station. As wealthy benefactors, they had reputations to maintain in the community.

Chief Teague sat them down on opposite sides of a big Formica table, one where they couldn't get at each other. He didn't want to have to break up a fight between two grown siblings.

"Now here are the rules," Harry Teague said. "This meeting is off the record. You work things out, we can drop any charges. You don't, there will be serious consequences. It's up to you."

And so they began to spin their falsehoods.

~ ~ ~

"My brother accidentally shot me," N.L. Purdue lied smoothly. "I don't intend to press any charges."

Bobby Ray nodded. "That's right, like Newcombe says, it was an accident. I'm not used to handguns. I must have pulled the trigger without meaning to."

"Yes," nodded the older man. "He was showing me that revolver he'd recently bought. Said it was a collector's item."

Bobby Ray matched his brother's prevarication. "As everybody knows, I'm a collector. Juke boxes, comic books, rare coins – even guns. That one was a real find."

"Where did you buy it?"

"Barney Brown's Pawn Shop over in Burpyville. Big Nose Barney knows to call me when he comes across an interesting item. I pay top dollar for things that interest me."

"And you found this gun interesting?"

"That's right," nodded Bobby Ray. "First manufactured in 1930, the Enfield No. 2 was the standard British Empire sidearm during the Second World War. Even so, they're fairly hard to come by these days. I got a good buy on it."

"So, tell me," probed the Police Chief, "why did you bury such a valuable gun in a box?"

"After accidentally harming my brother, I wanted nothing further to do with that pistol. I decided that burying the gun was an easy way to get rid of it. Little did I expect the Quilters Club would take up gardening in my backyard."

Chief Teague waved him silent. "Are you willing to drop any trespassing or other charges against those fine ladies or anyone else involved in retrieving that box?"

"Hmm, I'll have to think about that. Maybe talk to my lawyer. They did invade my privacy. And they absconded with my property."

"Technically, that willow tree is on Cookie Bentley's land that surrounds your property," replied the Police Chief. "And one could argue you had abandoned that box."

This gave Bobby Ray pause. "When you put it that way, Harry, of course I'll drop any charges. That is, if you in turn drop any charges against me for discharging that firearm."

"I'm willing to do that if that's what your brother wants."

"It is," Newcombe Purdue gave a curt nod. He was sitting as straight as a stick, his suit freshly pressed, the only thing out of place being his arm in a medical sling.

"All right, this matter is cleared up then. Everybody walks away, the *status quo*."

"Very good," said Newcombe.

"Yes," agreed Bobby Ray.

The Police Chief held up a finger to get their attention. "Before you go, I have one little question to ask. Off the record, of course."

"Shoot," said Bobby Ray, then grimaced. "Bad choice of words," he admitted. "I mean, go ahead."

"Why did you try to kill your brother.

Bobby Ray flinched. "Off the record?"

"Off the record."

"When I was five years old, he took away my tricycle. I'll never forgive him for that, the big bully."

"That was over three decades ago. Isn't that a long time to hold a grudge?"

"Yes, I thought I was over it," said Bobby Ray. "But he invited me to dinner last week and we got to talking about old times, our boyhoods. I brought up the tricycle incident and he laughed about it. Said he'd do it over again if he had the opportunity. I'm afraid I saw red. I had the Enfield No. 2 with me, so I shot at him but missed."

"You didn't miss," frowned his brother. "You hit my shoulder."

"I was aiming for your head."

"You were irresponsible with that tricycle. Running all over mother's flower bed. I dumped it in the swamp. Good riddance."

"That was *my* trike. You had no right!"

"You were always a brat. You haven't changed one iota."

"Oh yeah?" Bobby Ray stood up, fists balled like twin cudgels. He was ready to fight.

N.L. leaped up, waving his cane like a club. "You deserve a good thrashing," he shouted.

"Bring it on, Big Brother!"

"You asked for it —"

"Hold on, you two hotheads," ordered the Police Chief. "Don't forget why you're here – to bury the hatchet. One more word from either of you and I'll throw you into matching jail cells."

"On what charge?" demanded one of the brothers.

"Disturbing the peace," said Chief Teague. "My peace."

# CHAPTER THIRTY-ONE

## The Big News

N'yen Madison finished his article on the Voyager space flights and pressed the key to send the Microsoft Word document to his editor. It swooshed away like those cylinders in pneumatic tubes at bank drive-throughs – off to *Scientific American*'s offices on West 40th Street in New York City.

"Next?" he consulted his notes. Here was an idea for a piece about Space X versus Blue Origin. Or an idea about a mysterious blinking light in Deep Space. Or one about enlarged hot spots on the Sun.

Hmm.

Just then the phone rang. He could see that it was his wife calling from the library. "What's up, Cupcake?" he answered it with a smile.

"Oh, sorry to disturb you, N'yen," came a voice he recognized as Tessie Humphrey, the assistant librarian. "But you better come over to the library. Sissy fainted, but she's refusing to let me call a doctor."

"I'll be there in five minutes," he said, not even bothering to close down his computer.

~ ~ ~

When N'yen Madison rushed through the library's wide glass doors, he spotted Sissy sitting at a table near the coffee kiosk, sipping on a latte. Tessie was hoovering nearby like a mother hen, leaving the front counter unattended.

"Sissy, you all right?" he gushed.

"Sit down," she commanded.

He did.

"This isn't how I planned to tell you," she said, taking his hand. "But you're going to be a daddy."

That's when N'yen fainted.

~ ~ ~

"That's great news," exclaimed Aggie when she heard. "I'm so happy for you guys." And she was. Her two best-est friends starting a family. She was sure they would ask her to be the godmother.

Sissy grinned. "I'm only a month along, according to a GYN over in Burpyville. I've only known for three days now. But I'm getting morning sickness. That sucks."

N'yen looked more shaky than his wife. "This is great – if unexpected – news," he squeaked.

"I wonder what an Afro-Asian will look like," said Tessie, standing back to give Sissy room to breathe. She didn't mean to be racist or anything like that. It just that around this part of Indiana, everybody was plain vanilla.

"She will be beautiful," declared Sissy.

"S-she?" stammered N'yen.

"That's just my guess. Technically, it's too soon to tell."

"They will give you a sonogram at about 14 weeks," said Aggie, as if she were an expert on child birthing and such. "That might tell you."

"I suspected you might be preggers," said Tessie. "I could hear you throwing up in the restroom. At first, I thought it might be food poisoning, bad oysters or something. But after four mornings in a row, I was pretty sure what was going on."

"After a few mornings like that, I went down to Kupnick's Pharmacy and bought a pregnancy test. Peeing on the stick gave me the answer right away. Doc Medford recommended a good GYN over in Burpyville. Dr. Martha Greenwood – I like her a lot."

"So those weren't shopping trips?" muttered N'yen, putting the pieces together.

"Of course not," said Aggie. "If those were shopping trips, she would have taken me along. I'm a talented shopper, you know."

"That you are," agreed Sissy, sharing a high-five.

"I never pass up an SO," said Aggie.

"An SO?" repeated N'yen with a furrowed brow.

"A Shopping Opportunity," translated his wife.

"Have you told your mother and grandfather?" asked Aggie. Sissy's mother had come to live with them a few years ago. Miraculously, the former druggie had been clean ever since. Part of the deal was she had to submit to regular testing.

"You guys are the first to know – other than the doctors."

"Buck's going to be thrilled to be a great-granddad," predicted N'yen. "But I'd bet he'll be praying for a boy."

"We'll see about that," grinned Sissy. "He was pretty happy raising me."

"Grammy's going to be excited," said Aggie. "I'll bet she starts quilting a baby blanket before the week is out."

# CHAPTER THIRTY-TWO

## Opening the *Ajna*

Adivaita Nelson found her husband's uncle to be a strange person. He made his living exhibiting damaged people, although the ones she had met seemed quite happy with the arrangement.

Her familiarity with Pete McGuffey's livelihood had prepared her for the recent meeting with that man with three eyes. The Hindu belief in a third eye – the *Ajna* – was one thing; seeing an actual eyeball in the middle of someone's forehead was another.

The third eye is considered to be the sixth chakra (wheel-like energy centers) in the body. It is believed to be linked to the pineal gland, a pea-sized gland shaped like a pine cone, located in the brain near the hypothalamus and pituitary gland. This is a revered tool of seers and mystics. It's sometimes called the Sixth Sense.

Hindus believe that the third eye is a window to the spiritual world. Sometimes Addy felt that her *ajna* had opened to provide her with a clearer vision.

There were ways for believers to determine this.

**6 Signs To Know That Your Third Eye Is Open**

> 1. Heightened Intuition. You might experience a sudden increase in intuitive insights and gut feelings, guiding you in decision making and daily life with accuracy.
> 2. Vivid Dreams and Vision.
> 3. Sensitivity to Energies.
> 4. Increased Psychic Abilities.
> 5. Heightened Awareness.
> 6. Synchronicities.

Addy followed these signals carefully. She was sure her *ajna* had come awake on several important occasions during her adult life.

If one could only control it!

Now, she tried to exercise this inner power, to open her third eye to heighten her awareness, increase her psychic abilities. She felt that Randolph Johnson was a harbinger of some arcane message. Perhaps if she cleared her mind and opened her eye, she could divine why Shiva had sent this odd man to her.

Addy sat quietly in her living room, her mind easing into a meditative state. She tried to focus her *ajna* on Randolph Johnson, picturing him in her mind, trying to connect with his essence. It was close to a hypnotic trance.

Perhaps she fell asleep. Perhaps she dreamed.

Somehow it came to Adivaita Nelson that the "angel" Randolph Johnson had seen was none other than the human form of Shiva the Destroyer. Of course, this god was a destroyer, the lord of the cosmic dance, and the lord over all beasts.

Th etymology of Shiva is with the Sanskrit root *śarv-*, which means "to injure" or "to kill." That suggested this supposed angel was a killer, somehow involved in Fritz Berber's death.

Addy phoned Police Chief Harry Teague to share her insight. He was very polite, but dismissive. "We have the killer, ma'am. No question but what Birdie Longstreet pulled the trigger. Her doorstep, her gun, her fingerprints on the gun, her confession."

She felt like a fool. Obviously, the lawman did not know how Shiva worked, influencing events rather than direct intervention.

"But didn't Randolph Johnson tell you he saw someone else at the scene of the death?"

"Oh, you mean the angel?"

"That's right."

"I didn't know Buddhists believed in angels."

"I am Hindu. About half of them believe in angels. Buddhists, not so much."

"Well, I guess we Baptists believe in them too. But I'd have a hard time convincing a court of law that Fritz Berber's death was caused by divine intervention."

"You do not understand me. I am saying that another man was involved – whether you think he was moved by a deity or not. Randolph saw him. That's why Mr. Berber was trying to get inside Mrs. Longstreet's house, as a sanctuary from this threatening figure, this dark angel, this destroyer."

"Three Eyes Johnson is not the most reliable of witnesses. Are you aware he thinks he has a twin brother living inside him."

"Medically, that may be true. He has what doctors call a parasitic twin."

Chief Teague sighed. "Gotta admit, that extra eyeball of his does seem to operate on its own, looking right and left while his own eyes are looking left and right."

"So you will try to locate this dark angel?"

"We'll sniff around. But finding him won't change the fact that Miss Birdie's the one who shot her mailman."

# CHAPTER THIRTY-THREE

## The Bassball Bat

**N**ormally, Aggie would have been asleep for hours by now, but she was keyed up from Sissy's announcement earlier that day. It boggled her mind that she was going to become an "aunt."

That's when she heard the creak of her front door swinging open. Grampy had promised to apply some WD-40 to those noisy door hinges, but hadn't got around to it yet.

His procrastination had prompted Aggie to buy him a sweatshirt that proclaimed:

**IF I SAID I'LL FIX IT**
**I WILL**
**THERE IS NO NEED TO REMIND ME**
**EVERY SIX MONTHS.**

Aggie heard the squeak of hinges again. She lay very still, listening. Yes, she was sure there were footsteps in the living room. She had an intruder.

Easing out of bed, she picked up the baseball bat she kept propped against her bureau. It was a 25-inch hickory Louisville Slugger. The hardest wood available for a bat, rarely used anymore.

Barefoot, she tiptoed down the hallway. She could see a shadow moving about the living room, piling her flat screen TV and Blue Dog painting and new iPad in the center of the floor. As he bent over to add a porcelain vase to the booty, she stepped forward and swung the bat. She aimed for his shoulder, careful not to hit his head.

*Whack!*

"*Ow-eee!*" came the scream. "You broke f-ing my arm." The figure hopped about, a dark silhouette that could have been a Potawatomi Indian doing a war dance.

Aggie flipped on the light switch, keeping the baseball bat at the ready. Her next blow – if need be – would take out a kneecap.

"Ow, ow, ow," continued the howling.

"Gus Bentley, what are you doing here in my house in the middle of the night?" she demanded, obviously surprised at the identity of the intruder.

"Ow," he grunted, clutching his right arm with his left hand. "I think you broke my arm."

"That's not all I'll break if you don't start talking."

"Ow, ow. I was just prowling around for the fun of it."

"Looks like you were helping yourself to my TV and iPad."

"Those were just trophies, proof that I'd been here."

"Gus, you're a police deputy, not a cat burglar."

"I know, I know. I was just having a little sport."

"Were you the one who broke into N'yen Madison's house last week, took his TV set."

"Yeah."

"How did you manage that? You were at Birdie Longstreet's house. That was the day she shot the mailman."

"I did N'yen house in the morning, before Birdie shot the mailman. N'yen was locked away in his room, music blasting, he didn't hear a thing."

"About that TV set and crystal punchbowl ...."

"I'll give 'em back. I have 'em at home. Stashed in the barn. Not like I'm selling the stuff I took."

"Hmpt, that's no excuse. Stealing is stealing. Burglary is burglary."

"Geez, I was only having a little fun."

"Best you place yourself under arrest. I'm phoning Chef Teague."

"He'll be ticked off if you get him outta bed this time if night."

"He'll be ticked off that one of his deputies is breaking into people homes."

"Guess I'm toast. Harry Teague will fire me."

"You may do a little jail time too."

"Once a Crackleton, always a Crackleton. Don't know what made me do this. Bad genes, most likely."

"Bull poop. I've got Crackleton genes too. You don't see me acting like a hooligan. Aunt Cookie's gonna be very disappointed in you."

"Yeah, I've let her down f'sure. What was I thinking?"

Taking that as a rhetorical question, she didn't bother replying. "Okay, here's what we're going to do," she continued. "We're not going to tell Chief Teague about this. You will return all the stolen stuff to N'yen. He and I won't press any charges. You will tender your resignation as a deputy, find a new job. And you will tell your mom about this, but no one else. She deserves to know what a skunk you've turned out to be."

"Okay, okay. I'll do all that. And I'll straighten up and fly right. No more breaking and entering for the fun of it. Now will you take me over to Doc Medford's to get him to look at this arm. I'm sure it's broken."

# CHAPTER THIRTY-FOUR

## Repentance Required

Augustus Crackleton – known these days as Deputy Gus Bentley – was next in line as heir to the Ben Bentley land fortune. His adopted mother had doubled its value since Ben died. But Gus still had that tainted Crackleton blood surging through his veins. To put it bluntly, he was a "thief at heart."

Sure, he was the one who had burgled N'yen and Sissy's house last week, more for the thrill of it than the goods he had taken. He didn't need another TV set and certainly had no use for a punch bowl.

And now he'd been caught breaking into Aggie Tidemore's home. That was a bummer.

His confession nearly broke Cookie Bentley's heart. She had loved Gus as her own ever since the little six-toed boy came to live with her and Ben. She was so grateful to N'yen and Sissy for refusing to press charges. Aggie too.

"I'm very disappointed in you," Cookie told him.

"Sorry, Mom," mumbled Gus, head down, hands deep in his pockets.

"You owe Aggie a big thank you," she added.

"For breaking my arm?"

"Doc said it's only bruised. No, you owe her a thank you for not turning you in. You would be facing jail time."

"Can I get one of the farm hands to help me get N'yen's TV and stuff out of the barn. Best I return it to him so he won't press charges neither."

"Sure. But after that you go down to the police department and resign. Just tell Harry that you've decided you're not cut out for police work."

"Yes'um."

~ ~ ~

When Aggie told him about her run-in with a burglar (she didn't identify the intruder's name), N'yen was glad he had installed a new Silver Bells security system at Melon Rind House. It paid to be vigilant, he assured himself. Being robbed once was plenty enough for him.

But the more N'yen thought about the guy who put in the alarm – Earl Kyle Brown, his card had said – the more misgivings he had. Not only did the guy have shifty eyes, that extra digit on his left hand identified him as a Crackleton.

Careful now, N'yen told himself. He didn't want to be too judgmental, assuming that all Crackletons were bad – but he had to admit that was a pretty good rule of thumb.

Sure, his cousin Aggie was a Crackleton – well, 1/8 by his calculation – and he trusted *her* with his life. But he couldn't extend that confidence to this guy Earl Kyle Brown.

Just to be cautious, N'yen phoned his Aunt Cookie. Before retiring, she had maintained the genealogy charts for the Historical Society. With her eidetic memory, she knew them backwards and forwards. She could recite the family tree for 'most anybody in the town.

"Earl Kyle Brown is a Crackleton, alright," she confirmed N'yen's suspicion. "He and his brother Barney are Crackletons by way of their mother, one of Granny Crackleton's daughters."

"Are these brothers shady characters?" He was careful with his words, knowing her adopted son Gus was a Crackleton by birth.

"Shady? Both have done jail time, if that's what you're asking. Earl Kyle for attempted burglary; Barney for possession of stolen goods. Barney runs a pawn shop over in Burpyville. Earl Kyle operates a security service – sorta like letting a fox into the hen house, I'd say. We declined to use that alarm system at the Perricock Museum. Too risky."

"Thanks, Aunt Cookie. You've been helpful."

"Tread carefully, if you have a Silver Bells security system. By my calculation, an inordinately high number of homes with Silver Bells Security have been burglarized." That freak memory enabled her to compute statistics like an IBM quantum computer on steroids. "About four percent of their customers get burglarized each year. The national average is only one quarter of one percent. The difference is suspicious, wouldn't you agree?"

"That's very convincing," he agreed. "Sixteen hundred times the national average. You'd be safer without a Silver Bells alarm system."

"My point exactly."

"I need to give this some though," he said.

After wrestling with his concerns for a night or two, N'yen Madison phoned his pal Tommy Truehart. "Hey, Kemosabe, would you do me a favor? I want you to check out my home security system, make sure it's on the up and up."

"No problem," said Tommy. "You should have had me install it in the first place."

~ ~ ~

Aggie decided to take her own advice and get a dog. Her longtime pooch had passed away a few years ago, now laid to rest in the pet section of Pleasant Glade Cemetery. After all these years, Tige had finally been allow into the boneyard.

At Strays & Others, she found another wire-haired dachshund, not much of a guard dog, but cute as the dickens. She named him Tige Two, deciding to call him Two for short. Not a replacement for her old doggie, but a successor as it were.

At least the little mutt would provide an alert if any other intruders broke into her house. She was normally a sound sleeper; it's a wonder she'd heard Gus Bentley's stealthy entrance.

Strays & Others had bent the rules, letting her take the doggie home before he'd received all his shots. She'd promised to come back in a few days to complete the process.

Marybelle Olsen was running the animal shelter now that Aunt Bootsie had moved to Florida. Marybelle's vacating her position at the retirement home had made way for Benjamin Nelson as its new director.

# CHAPTER THIRTY-FIVE

## New Circus in Town

Professor Pete McGuffey was standing next to his *Cabinet of Curiosities* truck when Addy got home from the supermarket. Tuesday was Food Lion's Two-for-One produce specials. She was surprised to see the Professor talking with two very bizarre people. One she recognized as Randolph Johnson; the second, a woman with a slanted, undersized head that was topped by a tuft of purple hair. She was one of his performers, no doubt.

"Oh, there you are," her husband's uncle greeted her. "I misplaced my key. I'm locked out of the house."

"No problem. I have my key right here," she held up a shiny object for him to see. "Perhaps you and your friends will help me carry the groceries in."

"Happy to." He waved at his companions. "I think you know Three Eyes," he said. "And this is his sister Babs. She works with the show. And I'm about to sign Randolph for the next season as our star attraction."

"How nice."

"I've decided this is gonna be my last season on the road. So I plan to go out with a bang. Adding Three Eyes. And there's a guy down in Philly I hope to sign. He has four arms."

"Like Vishnu. He has four arms, two in front symbolizing his presence in the human world and two in the back for his relationship with the spiritual realm. In his hands he hold four symbols: the conch, the chakra, the club, and the lotus flower."

"Say, that's a great idea. I will promote the guy as a genuine Hindu god, four arms and all. Dress him like a maharaja."

"I'm not sure that would be proper."

"Proper-topper – a sideshow ain't supposed to be proper. That's what the rubes come to see, that which would be improper to gawk at under different circumstances."

"I see."

"Now, can we use your dining room table to sign the contracts. I'm going to make Three Eyes a big star."

"You don't mind, I'll need to look through the contract one more time before he signs," Babs reminded him.

"No problem." The Professor turned to Addy, "Babs here is Randolph's manager. You wouldn't know it to look at her – with that pointy head and all – but she's a sharp businesswoman. I have her do my taxes on the side."

Babs smiled modestly. "Most people think my brain inside this tiny head is stunted or something. Gives me an edge on most people I do business with."

"She's smart," nodded Three Eyes. "Tells me I don't need two contracts, one for me and one for Rex. Saves a lot of paperwork."

~ ~ ~

Aggie got a call back from J. Walter Grisham of Grisham Grisham & Bartholomew in Indianapolis. "We've drawn up the papers for Mr. Purdue's purchase of two hundred acres of land abutting the Wabash River from your client, one Katherine Ann Johansson Brown Bentley. I am emailing you a draft for your perusal. Once we agree on the details, I will messenger the finished document for Mrs. Bentley to sign. You know the routine, I assume."

That comment probably meant he'd looked her up and discovered that she'd been a member if the bar for about ten seconds. Nonetheless, she held her own. "Send the pdf whenever you're ready. I'm sure we can complete this transaction before the end of the week."

"Excellent. And that price is correct?"

"It is."

"I'm not trying to negotiate against my client's interests, but the amount seems rather low."

"That's Mrs. Bentley's price. She doesn't need the money."

"That's what Bobby Ray said."

"But I believe he's supposed to buy an elephant as part of the deal."

"An elephant?"

"Yes, you know. An animal that looks like a hippopotamus with a sock on his nose."

"I believe I can recognize an elephant when I see one."

"So can Bobby Ray. He used to work in a circus before he got rich."

~ ~ ~

"Fifty percent. Ain't that a lot to be my manager?" frowned Randolph Johnson.

"Not really," replied his sister Babs. "That's twenty-five percent for you; twenty-five percent for your brother Rex."

"Oh. That makes sense."

Professor McGuffey spoke up: "Hurry it up, my boy. Sign those papers. You'll need to go home and pack. We'll be heading out right away. Got a four-armed man in Philly to sign."

"Yessir." He bent over the contract, making his signature with a careful scribble.

"That-a boy," encouraged his sister.

"By the way," said Three Eyes when the paperwork was finished, "I saw that angel again."

"You did? Where?"

"Over at the circus."

"What circus? Do you mean that petting zoo north of town."

"Nope. I mean that big red and blue and yellow tent where the Kensingers' house used to be."

# CHAPTER THIRTY-SIX

## Less Like a Crackleton

Buck Jackson was happier than a big black bear in a honey tree to learn that his granddaughter was expecting. Sissy's mother was thrilled too. Already, she was collaborating with Maddy Madison and Aggie Tidemore on a baby shower.

N'yen didn't know what to make of his changing status – from boy genius to expecting dad. In his early twenties, he was certainly old enough to be a father. But his appearance was that of someone hardly old enough to be in long pants.

He supposed he should buy a box of cigars and hand them out to his friends. Wasn't that the tradition? However, being a non-smoker, he wound up buying bubblegum cigars like you'd find in a candy store. Everyone appreciated his sense of humor.

As Freud said, "Sometimes a cigar is just a cigar."

~ ~ ~

Benny Nelson dearly loved his wife, but sometimes Adivaita's Indian mysticism could be exasperating. Case in point: the way she was conflating the god Shiva with that three-eyed freak Randolph Johnson.

But Benny kept his mouth shut. His uncle had built a business around people like Three Eyes Johnson, oddities of nature that attracted the curiosity of so-called normal folks. The Professor's sideshow allowed them to turn a handicap into a source of income. They took pride in their ability to entertain.

Some of them made pretty good money too. The weirder the deformity, the bigger the bucks. The Professor was offering Three Eyes a six-figure salary to join McGuffey's Cabinet of Curiosities. That was considerably more than the man had made as a "scout" for Big Ed Crackleton.

As Babs explained it to her little brother, "C'mon, Randolph, you're ready for the Big Time."

Being Three Eyes Johnson's manager, she would take a usurious 50%. After all, that's the percentage Col. Tom Parker got of Elvis Presley's earning. Besides, Three Eyes wasn't good with money. He'd never know the difference.

~ ~ ~

Granny Crackleton had a few choice words for Gus. A relative or not, nobody did petty crimes in Caruthers Corners without her or her brother Ed's okay.

"A broken – or bruised – arm will be the least of your worries, you do something stupid like that again," barked the old witch woman. "You want to work for Ed's crew snatching purses, just speak up. But we don't tolerate freelancing in this family."

"But –"

"No excuses. You barely qualify as a Crackleton no more anyway, getting adopted out to that hoity-toity Bentley family. You'd best toe the line, boy, if'n you know what's good for you."

Gus didn't like the way Granny has spoken about his mom –adopted mom, that is. Hoity-toity indeed! Cookie

Bentley was the kindest, most generous, bests mother one could possibly hope for.

The more he thought about it, the less he felt like a Crackleton.

# CHAPTER THIRTY-SEVEN

## Text Exchange

Beelzebub666 sent an encrypted text to his pal N'yen Madison. It said:

>WHILE YOU'VE BEEN PROCREATING I'VE BEEN DIGGING INTO IVOR MUSCOVY'S BACKGROUND. HE WAS IN WITNESS PROTECTION BECAUSE KGB MURDER SQUADS WERE HUNTING HIM DOWN. IF I DIDN'T KNOW MISS BIRDIE KILLED HIM I'D SUSPECT THE RUSKIES.

N'yen replied right away:

>THE KOMITET GOSUDARSTVENNOY BEZOPASNOSTI WAS DISBANDED IN 1991. IT WAS SUCCEEDED BY THE FEDERAL SECURITY SERVICE (FSB).

Tommy was irked by that correction.

>YES, BUT SLANG USAGE OF KBG PERSISTS. IN 2006 THE FSB WAS GIVEN THE LEGAL POWER TO ENGAGE IN TARGETED KILLING OF TERRORISM SUSPECTS OVERSEAS IF ORDERED BY PRESIDENT PUTIN.

N'yen responded:

>LIKE THAT UMBRELLA WHERE DISSIDENT WRITER GEORGI MARKOV WAS KILLED WITH RICIN BY THE BULGARIAN SECRET SERVICE ACTING ON BEHALF OF THE KGB.

Tommy added:

>OR SOVIET DEFECTOR ALEXANDER LITVINENKO WHO WAS THE VICTIM OF A LETHAL DOSE OF POLONIUM-210.

N'yen responded:

>THE RUSKIES LIKE TO SOLVE PROBLEMS WITH ASSASSINATIONS.

Tommy observed:

>THEY SEEM TO LIKE POISONING.

N'yen countered:

>BUT FRITZ BERBER/IVOR MUSCOVY WAS SHOT IN
THE HEAD BY A DOTTY OLD LADY.

Tommy countered:

>AUTOPSY SHOWS THE VICTIM HAD DDT IN HIS LUNGS.

That caught N'yen off guard:

>HOLY MOLY. YOU MEAN LIKE FLY SPRAY?

Tommy replied:

>ENOUGH OF IT IS TOXIC.

N'yen answered:

>WHAT ARE YOU SAYING?

Tommy had the last word:

>I THINK THE RUSKIES GOT TO HIM BEFORE
MISS BIRDIE DID.

~ ~ ~

Addy Nelson noticed the pretty blonde walking her dog down the street in front of her house. "Hullo," she called. "Aren't you Agnes Tidemore, the attorney? You helped on the closing when we bought this house."

Aggie pulled gently on the lease to signal for Two to stop. "Right, I did," she responded. "And you are Adivaita Nelson, aren't you?"

"Call me Addy. I'm trying to assimilate."

"Addy, then."

"I read in the newspaper that you are defending Mrs. Longstreet in the mailman's death."

"True," Aggie admitted cautiously. She didn't like to get drawn into conversations about her clients and current cases.

"You are aware there was a witness?"

"Yes, Three Eyes – uh, I mean Randolph Johnson. He said he saw it. I plan to take a deposition, but I'm not sure how reliable he will seem to a jury."

"Did you know he saw someone else at the scene of the death?"

Aggie tried to suppress her smile. "An angel, you mean?"

"Yes. That's how he described the person."

"Miss Birdie saw him too. She called him a Spaceman."

"Angel, Spaceman. They obviously saw the same person."

"The police haven't had much luck finding anyone who fits that description."

Addy gave her best cat-that-ate-the-canary smile. "I know where you can find him. Randolph saw him again – over at the Kensingers' house, the one that's being tented for termites."

# CHAPTER THIRTY-EIGHT

## Curb Service

Lydia Lazynski was having second thoughts. She should have let that Crackleton kid steal her prize quilt. That way she could have collected on the insurance. Her self-aggrandizing daughter had all her quilts insured. Lydia could've used the money. She didn't give a fig for those fancy patchwork quilts that had made her daughter famous.

Was it too late?

Mickey Mouse was in the custody of child services, but she knew Big Ed Crackleton had an army of underage thieves. That was his family business. She picked up the phone and called the Crackleton convenience store and left a message for Big Ed to give her a call.

By her calculation the insurance on the quilt – a valuable collectible – would cover her debt to Jeb Crackleton with enough left over to buy her a new TV set. She wanted one of those 70-inch HD flatscreens she'd seen at Walmart over in Burpyville. Her old Westinghouse was dying a slow electronic death. She needed a smart TV to avoid missing her "stories," as she called the daytime soap operas she followed as studiously as if spying on a neighbor.

The phone rang.

"Hello," she answered it.

"You called?" She recognized Big Ed's deep bass voice, his personal trademark.

"Come get the damn quilt. Your boy Mickey should've taken it rather than get himself caught like a bug in a roach motel."

"He's usually better."

"I'll be out this afternoon around three. I'll leave my front door unlocked."

"Happy to be of service."

"Does this make us even?"

"Even Steven."

"Excellent," Lydia Lazynski smiled. Her debt wiped out and she'd still be able to collect on the insurance.

~ ~ ~

That was before she spoke to the insurance company. They wanted an appraisal and a copy of the police report.

She had planned on jacking up the value, but an appraisal would lock it in at a fair price. Drat!

As for the police report, that would show the quilt hadn't been stolen. The police had thwarted an *attempted* robbery.

Could she report a second robbery? No, the police would never buy the idea of lightning striking twice in one spot. She was pretty sure Chief Teague had her number.

Was it too late to call Big Ed Crackleton and cancel their arrangement? No, that wouldn't work. Criminals had ways of dealing with people who reneged on a deal.

So, it turned out that she paid off a $600 loan with a $10,000 quilt. Guess there was truth in that old adage that crime didn't pay.

~ ~ ~

Tommy Truehart sat at his keyboard, typing furiously. He'd just turned up a new clue about the murdered mailman:

>MORE DIRT ABOUT IVOR MUSCOVY. RECORDS SHOW HE HAD A WIFE. SHE WAS PUT INTO WITNESS PROTECTION TOO.

Once N'yen Madison had breached the firewall for Fritz Berber's miliary records, Tommy Truehart had followed him through, doing more poking around. However, the information was sketchy.

>WHAT HAPPENED TO HER? FRITZ BERBER WAS SINGLE.

>MAYBE NOT. SHE MIGHT EVEN LIVE AROUND HERE. IT WOULD BE UNUSUAL TO SEPARATE A HUSBAND AND WIFE.

N'yen thought about that for a moment before replying:

>MAYBE SEPARATING THEM WAS A WAY TO THROW ANYBODY LOOKING FOR A COUPLE OFF THE TRAIL.

>MAYBE. BUT I DOUBT THEY WOULD HAVE AGREED TO A TOTAL SEPARATION. I THINK SHE IS HERE IN CARUTHERS CORNERS JUST LIKE HER HUSBAND.

>THAT IS A POSSIBILITY. WE JUST NEED A FEW MORE PIECES TO SOLVE THIS PUZZLE.

> ROGER THAT. I THINK WE ARE GETTING CLOSE.

>I BETTER TELL AGGIE. SHE MIGHT NEED THIS INFO AS PART OF HER DEFENSE OF MISS BIRDIE.

>DO THAT. I WILL KEEP SNIFFING THROUGH IVOR MUSCOVY'S FILES FOR A LEAD ON THE MISSING WIFE.

>DON'T GET CAUGHT. GOVERNMENT DATABASES HAVE LOTS OF SECURITY TRAPS TO PREVENT INTRUDERS FROM ACCESSING SENSITIVE RECORDS.

>DO NOT WORRY ABOUT ME. THEY WILL NEVER KNOW I WAS THERE.

Uh-oh, thought N'yen. Sometimes Beelzebub666 was too arrogant for his own good. That hubris was what allowed N'yen to constantly beat him when playing Tower Duel online. Overconfidence could do you in.

Last thing they needed was the Feds coming down on them for breaking into a classified database. But he knew there was no way of stopping Tommy when he made up his mind to do something. He'd either turn up Fritz Berber's wife ... or land them both in Federal prison.

# CHAPTER THIRTY-NINE

## The Tenting

Professor McGuffey said his goodbyes and assembled his caravan – the truck followed by three vans – preparing to head down to Philadelphia where he would sign Frankie the Four Armed Wonder (soon to be billed as Shiva the Hindu Deity) before joining up with Bob Bing's Three Ring Extravaganza for a week in St. Louis. After that, McGuffey's Cabinet of Curiosities would hook up with Barley's Big Top for the rest of the season – the Professor's Last Hoorah, as it were.

To get to Philadelphia, McGuffey had to find his way over to 21 East, but even with Babs Johnson's backseat driving he found himself taking a circuitous route through town. He fell in behind a little yellow Kia that seemed to know where it was going, but to his consternation it led him and his entourage to a side street where a house was being tented for termites. When the Kia pulled over in front of the house, he pulled in behind it, hoping to ask the driver for directions.

That was when Three Eyes Johnson, who was riding up front in the truck with the Professor and his sister Babs, began to hoot and holler like a madman: "It's him," he pointed. "It's the angel. This is where I saw him again."

~ ~ ~

Aggie had phoned Bobby Elwood to tell him she was dropping by the worksite. As an excuse, she said she was returning his pocket knife which had fallen under the seat of her car. Sometimes, making out in a small vehicle was like a game of Twister.

Bobby was standing out front as she pulled up. He was talking to a man in a bulky HAZMAT suit complete with goggles and twin spray tanks strapped on his back. It gave her pause. At first glance, the sun behind him, the two humps of the tanks looked like angel wings.

Bobby beamed when he saw her. "Aggie, this is Mikey, my new helper. Ignore his outfit. He just went inside the tent to check on how the gas is distributing through the rooms. The Kensingers had a pretty serious termite infestation. A wonder the old building is still standing."

"Mikey?"

"Mikhail Slovak at your service, madam." The man gave a stiff bow, restrained by the getup he wore. Almost formal in his behavior.

"Pleased to meet you," she returned the greeting. "Are you Russian?"

"No, no. I am from Poland. I am here on a Green Card."

Aggie cocked her head, a sign of curiosity. "Would you mind if I asked you a question about your work?"

"I am sure Bobby can answer questions about work better than me."

"This is about your schedule."

"All right, ask me anything."

"Mikhail, were you at Beatrice Longstreet's house when she shot the mailman?"

"Somebody shot somebody? I know nothing about that," he was saying as he started to back away.

169

Behind her, she heard the voice of Three Eyes Johnson yelling, "That's him. That's the angel who was chasing Fritz Berber, spraying him with that magic wand. And Fritz was banging on Miss Birdie's door, begging her to let him in. He was scared of this fallen angel. Fritz was running for his life."

Three Eye's shouts caught Mikhail Slovak's attention. "What is this crazy man saying?" he muttered, voice muffled under his protective face mask.

Aggie picked up on Three Eye's accusations. "Why were you chasing the mailman?" she asked Slovak.

That caught him off guard. "Uh, because I wanted to give him a letter to mail to my mother back in Novosibirsk."

"I thought you were from Poland."

"Yes, the Republic of Poland."

"But Novosibirsk is in southern Russia." She was pretty good at geography.

"I misspoke. I meant Bialystok."

"Didn't you just say you weren't there when Fritz Berber got shot?"

The burly man pushed his goggles onto the top of his head. "I was confused. I am an immigrant. I am not good with the language. And it is upsetting to be questioned about murders."

"What's in your tanks?"

"Fipronil in one. Bifenthrin in the other."

"Do you ever use DDT?"

"Not for termites."

"We don't use DDT at all," interjected Bobby Elwood. "I told you that the other night."

"Yes, but –"

At that moment, Three Eyes Johnson came running up, still screaming about Mikhail Slovak being a fallen angel. "It's him, it's him!" he kept repeating like a stuck record.

"Who is this monstrosity?" cried Mikhail Slovak, recoiling from the odd little man. "Tell him to stand back. He scares me. I think he may be an evil spirit."

"Easy, Mikey," said Bobby Elwood.

The man regained his equilibrium. "Am I being accused of something? I am uncomfortable with this conversation."

Aggie shrugged. "Just saying you were lying about not being there when Fritz Berber was shot. Randolph Johnson here saw you."

"It's him, it's the angel," babbled Three Eyes.

"Is this some kind of trap?"

"Only if you stick your foot in it."

"What are you saying?"

"That you were somehow involved in Fritz Berber's death."

"Why, you little –"

"Hold on there, Mikey," said Bobby Elwood, stepping between them. "This is my girlfriend you're talking to."

"Oh, yes, sorry. My apologies."

Aggie tried to continue. "But he –"

Bobby cut her off. "Aggie, thanks again for bringing my pocket knife. It's as genuine Buck. I'd hate to lose it. Why don't you run along now and I'll see you tonight."

"Say," called Professor Pete McGuffey, huffing over to join them, "can someone direct me to Route 21?"

# CHAPTER FORTY

## A New Club

It was almost like a Quilters Club meeting of yore, but this time it was Aggie, N'yen, his wife Sissy, and his online friend Beelzebub666 (Deputy Tommy Truehart, to the outside world).

To complete the picture, they met in the crafts room of the Hoople Quilting Heritage Museum. That's where the Quilters Club – Maddy Madison, Lizzie Ridenour, Cookie Bentley, and Bootsie Purdue, if you remember them – used to meet on Tuesday afternoons to sew and solve crimes.

Aunt Lizzie was curious about Aggie's request to use the room, but acquiesced when her goddaughter told her they were forming a club. Its description and stated purpose remained unsaid. And Lizzie knew N'yen wasn't much of a quilter. But she didn't ask any questions.

A large square worktable dominated the space. Cubicles stuffed with fabric scraps and fat quarters lined two of the walls. A gigantic hanging quilt took up the entirety of a third wall – a group project of the one-time Quilters Club. The door and a row of bulletin boards completed the fourth wall. The overhead skylight provided plenty of illumination, particularly on a sunny August afternoon like this.

The room brought back fond memories for Aggie and Sissy and even N'yen. Tommy looked around in wonderment, as if he'd followed Alice down the Rabbit Hole.

"Okay, we're no longer junior members of the Quilters Club," declared Aggie. "What say we call ourselves: The Quilters Club: Next Generation."

"Hey cool," grinned N'yen. "Like *Star Trek: The Next Generation*."

"Yeah, whatever," his cousin rolled her eyes.

Tommy spoke up: "Hey, do I have to learn how to make patchwork quilts?"

"No, you Neanderthal," laughed Sissy. "Not unless you have an interest in the sewing arts. That's just a front for our real purpose – solving crimes."

"But I already do that. I'm a police deputy, remember?"

"This is what you might call 'an extracurricular activity,'" Aggie explained. "We might take a few shortcuts that you're not allowed to do in your regular job as a police officer."

"Like what?"

N'yen offered the hint of a smile. "Like breaking into government databases."

Tommy Truehart gave a sigh of relief. "Oh, that's no big deal," he said. "I already do that too."

~ ~ ~

The newly formed quartet of sleuths agreed they needed to bring Police Chief Teague into the loop, but not tell him about The Quilters Club: Next Generation. He might think it was silly, a group of young twentysomethings playing detectives.

"Chief Teague will never approve of 'vigilantism,' " said Aggie. As a member of the Indiana Bar, she knew when she was stepping across the line. She had to be very, very careful or she might lose her license to practice law.

But as her father – the onetime high-powered lawyer known as Mark the Shark – had once said, "Doing what's right is more important than doing it the right way."

She just hoped he remembered that admonition if she ever got called to task. She'd be asking him to defend her. Luckily, he'd kept up his own law license.

~ ~ ~

Big Ed took care of his boys. If he didn't, they would desert him like flies around vinegar. His acts of larceny depended on a constant supply of minions. They had to be Crackleton progeny to qualify. His nephews and cousins were born to the task, lawfulness not being a familial strongpoint. And loyalty to the clan was a given. Nobody ratted on the family.

"Go get Mickey Mouse," said Granny Crackleton. "He didn't give you up. Time for him to come home."

# CHAPTER FORTY-ONE

## The Second Target

**H**arry Teague stared across his messy desk at his deputy and N'yen Madison. "A Soviet spy?" he said. "Here in Caruthers Corners? Our mailman, Fritz Berber?"

"That pretty much sums it up, Chief," said Tommy Truehart.

"How did you guys come by this information?"

"Off the record?"

"Okay, off the record."

"N'yen broke into a military database; then I did the digging. Fritz Berber was actually a Soviet defector, an MVD officer named Ivor Muscovy. He was in a federal witness relocation program. To protect him against Ruskie assassins."

"That's right," said N'yen. "He worked here for the Post Office for nearly twenty years. What better place to hide him than in plain sight as a government employee?"

Chief Harry Teague pursed his lips to give all this information more thought. "And how does this Russian assassin tie in with Fritz Berber's death. There's no question about Birdie Longstreet shooting him."

N'yen said, "I'm told the autopsy found DDT or some similar toxin in his lungs."

"You got that from Aggie Tidemore, I assume,"

"No comment. But Tommy and I think a Russian Directorate 13 assassin was trying to poison Ivor Muscovy, but Birdie beat him to it with her trusty .45."

"You're saying this assassin was Birdie's so-called Spaceman?"

Tommy nodded. "Right – and he was Three Eyes Johnson's Angel."

"More importantly, we think we've found him," said N'yen. "Or at least my cousin Aggie did. His name is Mikhail Slovak. He's working as a pest control guy with Bobby Elwood's company. That explains the spacesuit and googles. And the twin tanks on his back that Three Eyes mistook for angel wings."

Police Chief Harry Teague squinted doubtfully. "You say he's still working there?"

"He was as of yesterday, Aggie confirmed."

"That doesn't make sense. If he's completed his assignment with Fritz Berber – Ivor Muskrat, or whatever his name was – why hang around? Time to get out of Dodge." Harry Teague was secretly hoping the man was gone. As a small-town cop, he didn't relish going up against a professional Russian assassin. He'd read too many John le Carré books to want to try that.

"We think there's a second target," blurted Tommy Truehart, not able to hold back their discovery. "That's why he hasn't left. My deep dive into Ivor Muscovy's defection revealed there were two of them – a man and a woman – both placed into witness protection."

"Even so, she may be in some other city," said Harry Teague.

"Don't think so," argued N'yen. "They were married. Spied together, defected together, so I doubt they would want to be separated."

"But Fritz Berber was a lifelong bachelor, or at least he presented himself that way. Best we know, he didn't even have a girlfriend."

"Maybe he had a secret girlfriend," shrugged Tommy. "That's not hard to do. I've been seeing one of the Andrews sisters for nearly three years and nobody knows about it."

"Everybody knows about it," laughed Harry Teague. "Word is, those twins switch off and on with you, and you don't even know it."

"You mean I'm seeing Mary when I think I'm seeing Catherine?"

"That's what I hear."

"Dang."

" '*Double your pleasure, double your fun,*' " N'yen chanted the old Doublemint chewing gum jingle. "Truthfully, I don't see that you've got anything to complain about."

Tommy grinned. "Hmm, I get your point. Two sisters are better than one. Maybe I'll marry 'em both."

"*Tsk, tsk.* Polygamy is illegal in the State of Indiana," Chief Teague reminded him.

"There's always a catch," Tommy sighed.

"At any rate," the Police Chief continued, "for Ivor Muskrat's wife we'd be looking for a single woman about his age – late 50s to mid 60s – who moved to town about twenty years ago."

"A Russian?" said Tommy.

"Not necessarily," responded N'yen. "At least not in appearance. We had no idea that our friendly neighborhood mailman was a Russki."

Chief Teague nodded. "Right, they are great at infiltrating our society. Didn't either of you ever read Nelson DeMille's *The Charm School*?"

"I watched *The Amerikans* on TV," offered N'yen.

"Close enough."

"So what do we look for?" asked Tommy.

"Most single women in that age group are divorced or widowed," noted Harry Teague.

"Or claim to be," corrected N'yen. "The key filter is someone without long-term family ties to Caruthers Corners."

"Most folks around here have a lineage that goes back to that wagon train that broke down on the banks of the Wabash in 1829."

"That narrows it down," said N'yen. "We're looking for an outsider. Someone not born here."

"Hey, *you're* an outsider," said Tommy suspiciously "And you don't look like you're descended from anyone on that wagon train."

"No, but I've lived here off and on practically my whole life. So it's not likely I'm from Russia."

"That's true," agreed Tommy, taking in N'yen's light brown skin tone and the epicanthic folds of his eyelids. "Gotta admit you don't look Russian."

"Besides, he doesn't look like he'd be anyone's wife," Harry Teague pointed out. "Plus he's in his early 20s, not late 50s or 60s. Get with it, Truehart."

"Tommy, for somebody as smart as you, you're can be pretty stupid," snapped N'yen. Obviously exasperated by his friend's lapse in logic. He suspected Tommy's skill at playing Tower Duel was more intuitive than analytical. He played a good game, but rarely came out the winner.

The Deputy held up his hands in mock surrender. "Okay, okay. I was just trying to get into the hang of how to identify the other target. Sorry about that."

"Why don't we start by making a list of all the possible candidates we can think of," suggested N'yen. "See who's on it."

"Good idea," agreed the Police Chief, taking charge. He passed around legal pads and ballpoint pens. "Starting writing, boys. First one who IDs her gets a free steak dinner on me."

N'yen nodded. "Shouldn't be too hard to identify her, now that we know what we're looking for."

"That's right, " Tommy raced on. "And if we can figure out who she is, we'll know Mikhail Slovak's next target –"

"– and catch him in the act," N'yen completed the sentence.

Harry Teague held up a hand like a traffic cop. "Let's try to catch him *before* the act," he corrected. "We don't want to lose anymore of our citizens ... even if they're here under false pretenses."

# CHAPTER FORTY-TWO

## Knights of the Roundtable

Birdie Longstreet's nephew – well, actually her great-grand-nephew, her brother's kid's kid, or something like that – turned up on Aggie Tidemore's doorstep.

"You're Aunt Birdie's lawyer, right?" inquired the teenager. He had Birdie's long nose and pointed chin, so the relationship was obvious.

"That's right, and you are –?"

"Jefferson Davis Bronstein, but you can call me Jeffie. Everybody does. I'm Beatrice Longstreet's only living relative. My dad's dad was her brother, Nathan Bedford Bronstein. Everybody's gone now, except me. And Birdie, of course."

"Come in. My home office is the door to the right."

He took a chair facing her desk, looking somewhat nervous. "The Caruthers Corners Police contacted me yesterday. I got here as quickly as I could. I live in Wisconsin. That's where Birdie is from. But she's lived here since she married Gordon Lochinvar Longstreet close to eighty years ago."

"She must have married young."

"I think she was only fifteen or sixteen. I'm not really up on the family history. My parents died when I was eight, so Birdie's been my only connection to that side of the family.

My grandparents on my mother's side raised me – but I spent summers here with Aunt Birdie."

"What do you know about the case?"

"Chief Teague filled me in. Said she shot the mailman. Will she go to jail?"

"No, I plan to prove her innocence."

"Her innocence?"

"Yes, it was self-defense. We have witnesses."

"That's good. I'm not sure how Birdie would do on the stand. As you probably know, she has gone through most of her life in a slightly confused state."

"Slightly?"

"I see you know my aunt."

"It's clear she shot Fritz Berber as he tried to break into her house. The Castle Doctrine will prevail. We will try to keep her off the stand – claim health reasons or whatever. She has this fantastic story about Fritz Berber being a spy and that he belonged to some organization called The Knights of the Roundtable."

"Fritz Berber *was* a spy," stated Jeffie Bronstein. "But she's confused about the Knights of the Roundtable. What she meant is the KGB."

"KGB – that's the *Komitet gosudarstvennoy bezopasnosti,* the former Soviet Union's Committee for State Security. Right?

"No, but it has the same initials. It's actually a game called the Knights of Glory and Beer. KGB is an Internet multiplayer game that focuses on mass siege warfare and player vs player combat. Originally created in 1997, KGB has spanned several continents. It maintains a fairly elite gaming community."

"What's that got to do with Birdie Longstreet?"

"Nothing. It has to do with Fritz Berber."

Aggie's brow furrowed. "How so?"

"Fritz was a founding member. He inducted me during one of my summer visits. Fritz and I used to play KGB on a regular basis."

"Used to? You stopped?"

"Birdie insisted. She didn't trust online games. Said playing KGB would rot my brain."

Aggie stifled a laugh. Playing online games certainly hadn't diminished the brainpower of her cousin N'yen or Tommy Truehart. She pressed on: "What do you know about Fritz being a spy."

Jeffie politely corrected her. "Technically, he was a Soviet defector, not a spy *per se*."

"How did you know?"

"He told me himself. We grew very close, playing KGB together all those years. But he swore me to secrecy."

"Then how did Birdie find out?"

"I told her. I'm not good at keeping secrets. Mr. Blabbermouth, that's me."

"Birdie had me review her will recently. You are her sole heir, you know."

"I assumed so."

"That's how the police knew to contact you. I had your name and address. I wasn't surprised when you showed up at my door."

"No, you didn't look all that surprised."

"Have you seen Birdie yet?"

"I'm headed over to her house next. But I wanted to meet with you first and get the lay of the land."

"Birdie's fine. I will keep her out of jail. But pretty soon you may want to consider home care for her. Or moving her to the Hoople Retirement Center. That's the big building on the hill facing the Perricock Museum."

"Yes, I suppose so. But I'd only do that because of any physical infirmities. As for her mind, she's always been a few cards short of a full deck. That's what I've always loved about her; she saw the world through a unique filter."

"Did you know Fritz had a wife. She was in the federal witness program too."

"No, I didn't. But it doesn't surprise me."

"Why not?"

"He once mentioned that he'd been separated from the love of his life. But he said she was nearby. 'Waiting for him on a hill,' as he put it."

"On a hill? There are only two hills near here – sites of the Museum and the retirement home."

"Then that's where I'd look if you're trying to find her."

# CHAPTER FORTY-THREE

### Big Ed Steps Out

"Got a visitor," Elvira announced. In addition to being the police dispatchers, she and her sister Myrtle presided over the front desk.

"Send 'im in," called the Police Chief from his small office, only a few steps from where Elvira sat.

"You sure?"

"Why wouldn't I be sure?" he called back.

"Because it's me," said Big Ed Crackleton, his immense form filling the doorway.

"Oh," said Chief Teague, at a loss for words. This would have been like John Dillinger visiting FBI headquarters.

"I came for the boy. What's it gonna cost me?"

"We don't sell prisoners, Big Ed. Besides, Mickey isn't here. Child custody has placed him in a temporary foster home."

"And where might that be?"

"Maddy and Beau Madison have taken him in ... for the time being. He has a court date next week."

"Hm, Maddy Madison, you say? That might be okay. She's family, of sorts."

"Will you or your lawyer be showing up in court in his behalf?"

"Don't have a lawyer. Do we need one?"

184

"Be a good idea. Burglary is a serious charge."

"We already got the quilt, you know. Lydia turned it over to us. Spoils of war, you might call it."

"That's between you and her."

"She wants to report it to her insurance company as stolen. But they won't pay her without a police report."

"Too bad. She hasn't reported a second burglary."

"An oversight, I'm sure. But that's her problem. I've got the quilt – and I got it fair and square."

"So, are you going to show up in court on Mickey's behalf?"

"Sure, why not? He's a good burglar. Hate to lose him."

"I'd like to remind you that burglary is a crime."

"No business of yours, long as we do it down in Pitsville or over in Geneva."

"For Mickey's court hearing, I'd suggest you bring a lawyer."

"Who? Horace Hutchinson works for the town. Serves as acting prosecutor, when one's need. He won't do."

"You could try Aggie Tidemore."

"Aggie – I'd forgot about her. She's only been back in town about ten minutes."

"There you go then."

"Yes, she will do fine. She's family of sorts, too."

# CHAPTER FORTY-FOUR

## Will the Bugs Take Over?

"**W**ell, I hope you're happy," Bobby Elwood fumed. "My new guy quit this morning. Now I'm shorthanded to take down the tent on the Kensingers' house."

"That's no problem," said Aggie. "Abram Wagler has lots of sons. I'm sure David and Zeke can bring in more brothers to help. Ephraim's a good worker. Ham and Lot, too."

"Yeah, well. I was hoping Mickey would be my field man. Truth is, I don't like spraying all those poisonous chemicals."

"Maybe you should consider changing careers."

"What? And let bugs take over the world?"

~ ~ ~

Chief Harry Teague had gone out to the Kensingers' house that was being tented by Elwood's Bug Busters. It *did* look something like a circus tent.

However, the trip was a bust. Mikhail Slovak had hit the road without even picking up his last paycheck. There was no forwarding address. Bobby Elwood said he had no idea where his former employee had gone.

Fleeing was a sign of guilt. Maybe Deputy Truehart was onto something with that story about Fritz Berber being a spy

in a witness protection program. That's what Birdie
Longstreet had said too. But how did she know?

~ ~ ~

Tommy Truehart turned in the list he and N'yen had
compiled of possible suspects in the search for Ivor Muscovy's
missing wife. This was a compilation of the names of single,
middle-aged women who were not locals. They had culled out
the duplicates, ranked them in order of most likely candidates
to least likely.

Many names on the list had been quickly weeded out.

• For instance, Brenda Sprunger – head cashier at
Dollar General – at first seemed viable. An older
blonde, she was single with no known Significant
Other. But turns out, she was a cousin of Sad Sammy
Hankins, a well-known watermelon farmer. He had
known her since childhood. Scratch her name.

• Marnie Zarn – a teacher's helper at Daisy Mouse
Kindergarten – fit the profile in many ways. Single,
came here from "out west," spoke fluent Russian. But
she was much too young to have a previous life as a
spy.

• Frances Morgan also made the list. Since moving here
about the same time as Fritz Berber, she had worked
on and off as a part-time waitress at Cozy Café. But
there were discouraging traits. A chatterbox, she
seemed much too talkative for a former spy.

• Bitsy Smoot was on the list too. A Sunday School teacher at Pleasant Meadows, she was a mousy woman who kept to herself. But everybody knows she has a secret crush on Rev. Kilroy. She hardly seemed the type to be a godless Communist.

• Patricia Ann Muskie – a docent at the Perricock Museum of Science and History. She was said to be a divorcee who moved here from New York City because she "liked the small-town life." Not much was known about her.

• Dorothy Stargazer – the town's former librarian – would have qualified, being both middle-aged and single, a woman not originally from around here. However, a few years ago, a DNA test had proven with 99.6% accuracy that she was the secret love child of Ernst Friedrich Hegler (better known as The Great Wizardini).

• Margarite Dockery Rutaberger – known to her acquaintances as Rita – was the former owner of Melon Rind House before moving to the Hoople Retirement Center. It was said she had retired after years with IBM in Chicago. But who knew for sure?

• Also, Marybelle Olsen qualified for the list, being a single lady of the right age. British, she had been the Hoople family's house manager and general factotum for many years. After the last of the Hooples passed away, she had done a stint as director of the new retirement home, but was now happily running the local Strays & Others animal shelter. Everybody agreed she was much too beloved by the townsfolk to be a serious contender for the list.

There were many others, but nobody who popped out like the femme fatale half of that *Boris & Natashia* cartoon.

Chief Harry Teague checked the list. It was longer than he'd expected. But nobody stood out. He wondered if they had already hit a dead end.

# CHAPTER FORTY-FIVE

## The Slow Deputy

**W**ith Gus Bentley's unexpected resignation, Chief Teague had been forced to bring Rufus Barnswell on full-time. The younger brother of high-school resource officer Benny Barnswell, Rufus had chosen to work part-time for years. Not exactly a get-up-and-go type, he eschewed having a regular workweek, but Harry Teague had pressed him into service with a raise.

As it happened, Rufus turned up the missing exterminator. Mikhail Slovak (if that was really his name) was found slurping a watermelon Blizzard at the DQ on South Main Street, not a hundred paces from the Caruthers Corners Police Department.

Rufus had taken a break, strolling up to the soft-serve stand for a parfait. He had a well-known sweet tooth, the prelude for the diabetes that would overcome him later in life. The cement tables and benches were communal, so he settled at a table facing a stony-faced man with a graying buzzcut. "Howdy, neighbor," he greeted his tablemate. "Ain't seen you 'round town before. What's your name?"

Mikey was caught off guard, focusing on his thick Blizzard. After all, Rufus wasn't wearing his uniform. Having worked only part-time, Rufus didn't have a backup when his khakis were at the cleaners. "Mikhail," he muttered matter-of-factly.

"Mikhail Slovak?"

"Who's asking?"

"The Caruthers Corners PD," he said, trying to snap the cuffs on the man's thick wrist.

"So you think, Barney Fife." With lightning speed, Mikey switched hands, leaving Rufus Barnswell handcuffed to the metal supports of the table.

"Hey!"

"See you around, Caruthers Corners PD."

And that's how Rufus lost his first-ever collar.

~ ~ ~

Aggie took her new dog back to Strays & Others because he was due one more shot: parvo. Dogs normally receive distemper, hepatitis, leptospirosis, parvo, and parainfluenza shots before being adopted out. Strays & Others had been temporarily out of parvo, but Marybelle Olsen had bent the rules, allowing Aggie to take home the dachshund if she promised to bring him back in a few days for the last of those DHLPP injections.

Parvo is a highly contagious disease caused by Canine Parvovirus Type 2. The virus attacks white blood cells and the gastrointestinal tract of dogs and other canids like coyotes, wolves, and foxes.

"Usually, we cover this with a 5-in-1 injection – but we just switched medical supplier so our inventory is a tad out of stock."

"I don't mind coming back. It gives me an excuse to see you." Marybelle Olsen had been like a second mother when Aggie was growing up in the Hoople Mansion (now the

Hoople Retirement Center). Her own mother had been a bit bonkers during those tender years, thinking she was a fairy princess. That had been a tough patch for Aggie.

Marybelle bent to examine the dog. She checked his ears, looked at his eyes, pried open his mouth, gave him a body pat down. "How's he working out?" she asked.

"Two is a good boy. While I'm here I want to buy a name tag for him."

"Two?

"Actually Tige Two. But Two for short."

"Just give me a moment here." She pulled out a syringe. "Hold still, Two."

"*Yip!*" the dog said as the needle pierced his skin.

"There, all done."

Aggie lowered her head close to the dog's. "See, boy, that didn't hurt. At least, not much."

Two licked her face with a wet tongue.

"Yuck-o. I just got a doggie facial."

"I can see you and Two will get along famously," smiled Marybelle.

"How about you? Do you like being director of the shelter?"

Marybelle shrugged. "I've always liked dogs and cats. But it has been a challenge. We all love Bootsie, but she was not one for organizing. The records are a disaster. The supplies were out of control. We have several dogs we're not sure where they came from."

"Anything I can do to help?"

"We need volunteers."

"Doing what?"

"Walking dogs. Cleaning cages. Washing blankets. Those kind of tasks."

"I can do that."

"Great. Can you handle Saturdays? I know you have a regular job, your new law practice and all."

"That works."

"Thank you, my dear."

Aggie looked at her friend more closely. "Are you okay? You seem kinda sad."

"Alas, I lost someone recently. I'm still grieving."

"Anybody I know?"

"No, no. Someone back in England."

"I'm so sorry."

"Life happens."

~ ~ ~

Gus Bentley was looking for a job. His mom – his adopted mom, that is – offered to let him help her manage the properties, but he wanted to stand on his own two feet. No more futzing around.

Granny Crackleton tried to talk him into joining one of Ed's crews, but he was through with stealing. He wanted to take a straight-and-narrow path from here on out. Make his mom proud of him.

His best bet was the Fire Department. He could handle that. Or – with a little training – maybe he could become a paramedic. Or work as a security guard at the retirement center.

He was going to change his ways.

Honest.

# CHAPTER FORTY-SIX

## Persons of Interest

**C**hief Teague narrowed the list down to one person of interest: Margarite Dockery Rutaberger.

Rita had moved here about twenty years ago, supposedly a widow. She claimed to have had a successful career with IBM, but Deputy Truehart could find no records of her employment with Big Blue. Maybe it was just a filing snafu. Maybe not.

Due to a broken hip, she had sold her old Victorian mansion known as Melon Rind House to N'yen and Sissy Madison, then moved into the Hoople Retirement Center. And hadn't Birdie's nephew suggested they should look for Fritz Berber's wife there in the retirement home on top of Hoople Hill?

The Police Chief eased his cruiser – the one donated to the town by Bobby Ray Purdue – slowly up the steep hill and parked in a slot marked **GUEST**. Benny Nelson met him at the front desk. "Rita's waiting for you in the parlor," said Benny. "You'll have privacy in there."

Chief Teague had called ahead, requesting to meet with Rita Rutaberger "for a confidential conversation." The old woman had agreed, seemingly eager to have company.

Harry Teague felt he was on the right track here. He'd learned from Mitty Ann Macintyre, who had lived next door to Melon Rind House for twenty years, that Fritz Berber would pause on his daily mail rounds to have tea with Rita Rutaberger. The remnants of a marital relationship?

Also, among Berber's personal belongings, he'd found a note the man had saved:

Thank you to the World's Greatest Mailman.
Rita

There could be a personal relationship there, the Chief told himself. Who wrote notes like that to their mailman?

Benny Nelson ushered Harry into the parlor where a gray-haired lady sat near the window. You could see the panorama of the town below, like a diorama in a museum.

The woman sat up straight, alert, a walking cane at her side. "Chief Teague," she greeted him. "I'm curious why you wanted to meet with me."

At that moment Harry Teague was wondering the same thing. This woman was quite elderly, likely in her late 80s or early 90s. Fritz Berber had been in his mid 60s, far too young to have been married to Rita Rutaberger.

"Uh, I'm just doing a background check. A request from your insurance company," he lied.

"Yes?"

"You moved her about twenty years ago?"

"That's right, when I retired from IBM. I worked in Chicago."

"Is that where you were born – Chicago?"

"No, no," she chuckled. "I was born here in Caruthers Corners. Used to play with the Hoople Quadruples – that's what we called them – when I was a girl. Then I went away to college, got a job with Big Blue, married, buried my husband, retired from IBM with a gold watch, returned home, bought

Melon Rind House, broke my hip, sold Melon Rind House, moved into this drafty old mansion, and here I sit receiving my first visitor – you. That's the story of my life, Chief Teague."

"Got it. That clears up any questions I had."

The old lady smiled. "I've enjoyed our talk. I hope you come again. It gets lonely up here."

~ ~ ~

Deputy Truehart had his own theory about the missing wife of Ivor Muscovy. He'd turned up her name in the military database – Anna Petrova Muscovy – but nothing about her new identity.

His theory was that a person in witness protection would choose an alternate name that was easy to remember. Slips could be deadly in the spy world. Wouldn't it make sense to pick the same initials? Or a similar given name? Or a name that reminded you of your previous identity?

Going back over the list that he and N'yen had compiled, one name stuck out – Patricia Ann Muskie. That to him seemed like a scrambled version of Anna Petrova Muscovy. Being a gamer, his mind worked like that.

While Chief Teague was visiting Rita Rutaberger at the Retirement Center atop Hoople Hill, Tommy was parking in the little lot beside the Perricock Museum of Science and History on the facing hill.

"Admission is one dollar," said the woman at the museum's entrance.

"I'm here on official business," said the deputy.

"Oh? Like what?" challenged the ticket seller, as if she suspected him of trying to cheat the museum out of its modest admission.

"I'm here to see Patricia Ann Muskie. I understand she's a docent here."

"Patty? Sure, but she's with a group tour right now. She should be back in –" she glanced at her wristwatch "–about ten minutes. You can wait over there," she nodded toward a wooden bench.

Tommy settled onto the hard seat of the bench and checked the email on his iPhone while he killed time. He deleted some spam, emailed Catherine Andrews asking her out on Saturday night, then texted N'yen Madison to tell him he'd identified Anna Petrova Muscovy.

His Vietnam buddy replied:

>WHO?

> PATRICIA ANN MUSKIE. KNOW HER?

>YES. BUT SHE CANNOT BE FRIZT BERBER'S MISSING WIFE.

>WHY NOT? SHE WAS ON OUR LIST.

>JUST LEARNED THAT OLD TOM DANCY IS HER UNCLE. SO SHE CANNOT BE A SOVIET DEFECTOR.

>THOMAS DANCY, THE TOWN CLERK?

>ONE AND THE SAME. PATTY MUSKIE IS HIS NEICE ON HER MOTHER'S SIDE. THAT'S WHY SHE MOVED TO CARUTHERS CORNERS.

>THEN SHE COULD NOT BE ANNA PETROVA MUSCOVY.

>THAT'S WHAT I AM TELLING YOU, BRO.

>OKAY, OKAY. IT WAS JUST A THOUGHT.

>YOU DO NOT WANT TO UPSET OLD TOM. HE HAS A LOT OF INFLUENCE ON POLICE DEPARTMENT PROMOTIONS.

>COPY THAT. OVER AND OUT.

Deputy Tommy Truehart quietly stood up and walked out of the building. "Back to square one," he muttered to himself as he started the cruiser and guided it down the steep roadway toward town.

# CHAPTER FORTY-SEVEN

## Bungled Burglary

**B**ig Ed Crackleton considered Caruthers Corners and a few surrounding towns his territory. He had three teams of miscreants – (a) burglars, (b) purse snatchers, and (c) pickpockets. All their activities were categorized as petty crimes, but it added up. The residents of Crackleton Crossing were well provided for by this illicit undertaking.

The burglaries were made particularly easy by the family's control of Silver Bells Security. That relationship allowed them to secretly open the doors of nearly 20% of the homes in the area.

Silver Bells' sister company – Barney Brown's Bail & Pawn – converted the stolen goods into cash. As a strict rule, the thieves did not keep any of the stolen goods. It was sold off as quickly as possible, low pricing assuring a rapid turnover. The items were rarely in their possession for more than 24 hours. Big Nose Barney had an active clientele list.

The local police were stymied.

What Big Ed didn't know was that the Brown brothers (his cousins, Earl Kyle and Barney) burgled a few houses on their own – giving them some extra off-the-books income. That was a no-no, but they were very careful how they went about it.

Big Ed didn't have a clue.

Among their targets were "protected" homes, people who were off-limits to Big Ed's teams. This included "relatives" like Maddy Madison and Maisie Walters, as well as fellow criminals (professional courtesy, as it were) and philanthropic institutions (like the museum and the retirement center). Even the Crackletons had standards.

Not so for Earl Kyle and Barney. A little skimming was a normal business practice for them.

~ ~ ~

A recent item in *The Burpyville Gazette* announced:

CARUTHER CORNERS, IN – Last week, local resident N'yen Madison was presented with the American Astronomical Society's Astrophysicist of the Year Award. In recognition of this honor, Mr. Madison received The Asti, a coveted trophy made of pure silver. The ceremony was held at the AAS offices in Indianapolis. "It is quite an honor," he said …

That's why Earl Kyle tried to break into N'yen Madison's house on a moonless night at the end of August. That trophy could be melted down and sold to a silver hoarder with little effort. Besides, the little snot had lots of other items that would move quickly in the pawn shop – telescopes, computers, Star Wars collectibles. And since this was a "protected" home – he was sort of a Crackleton relative by adoption – Big Ed would never miss Earl Kyle's take.

Breaking in was always a breeze. The laptop computer in the Silver Bells van could turn off a house's alarms, lasers, and video cameras with the *tap-tap-tap-tap* entry of a four-digit master code. Jimmying the lock on a side door was easy as pie for a guy like Earl Kyle Brown. As manager of the security company, he was also a professional locksmith.

But tonight, there seemed to be a problem. Try as he might, the computer would not override the alarm code. He tried entering it a dozen or more times without success. *Tap-tap-tap-tap. Tap-tap-tap-tap.*

Nothing.

How could that be?

He was still asking himself that question when the three police cruisers pulled up, blocking the van.

Chief Harry Teague stepped out of the Ford Police Interceptor Utility (PIU), a modified version of the Ford Explorer. He dangled a pair of handcuffs from one finger. "Ready to go to jail?" he smiled at Earl Kyle Brown.

"Hey, what's going on?"

"Deputy Truehart deprogrammed your security system and added feedback to alert us if anyone tried to unlock it. You know, to burglarize the place."

"I'm no burglar," Earl Kyle Brown protested. "I was merely conducting a test. Silver Bells regularly tests its customer systems."

"That's a load of bull excrement. We've got proof of your illegal activities."

"No way."

Chief Teague ticked off the facts as he slapped on the cuffs: "Last month, Tom Dancy's house was burglarized. It had a Silver Bells security system. A rare chess set was taken, among other items. That chess set turned up for sale in your brother's pawn shop. Burpyville Police had an undercover agent purchase the chess set and return it to Old Tom. We can document each stage of the robbery. A video camera on a shop across the street – a CCTV system maintained by one of your competitors – captured images of the Silver Bells van parked outside the Dancy house at the exact time the system went down. Also, it pictures you going in the kitchen door and coming out with the chess set and a handcarved jewelry box in your arms. We got you dead-to-rights."

"Says you. I want to speak to my lawyer."

"Sure, after we book you and get you comfortably settled into a jail cell. By the way, Burpyville PD is raiding Big Nose Barney's pawn shop at this very moment. They've been watching you guys for quite a while now. We were happy to cooperate. When N'yen Madison got suspicious of you, we rigged his alarm to let us know if anyone tried to disarm it. And here you are, caught in the act."

"That silver trophy ...?"

"Doesn't exist. With Mr. Madison's cooperation, we planted that squib in the Burpyville newspaper, hoping you might take the bait. And you did."

"Barney is also a bail bondsman. We'll be out by morning."

"Maybe you will. But the alarm company and the pawn shop will be permanently shut down. And I expect when your trial comes up, you and Big Nose Barney will be seeing a little jail time ... unless you turn state's evidence on your boss, Ed Crackleton."

Earl Kyle Brown looked indignant. "Rat out Big Ed? That'll never happen. We have what you might call a code of honor."

"In that case, I'd advise you boys to pack your bags for a long stay."

# CHAPTER FORTY-EIGHT

## Welcome to the Family

Aggie Tidemore stood before Judge Horace Cramer that bright September morning. Reluctantly, she had agreed to represent the Crackleton family re the disposition of twelve-year-old Mickey "Mouse" Crackleton.

After calling the court to order, Judge Cramer looked down at his docket. "I see we have a burglary charge against a minor."

Aggie spoke up. "Your honor, Mrs. Lydia Lazynski is not pressing charges."

"Is that so?"

At that moment, a figure stood up in the back of the courtroom. "If it please your honor, may I address the court," said Mark Tidemore, Aggie's Dad.

"Mr. Mayor?"

"Your honor, I am not here today in my capacity as mayor of Caruthers Corners, but as an attorney of record representing Madelyn and Beauregard Madison IV."

"Indeed? What have you – or they – to say in this matter?"

"I will let my clients speak for themselves, if the court permits."

"Proceed."

Maddy Madison stood up from her seat behind the defendant, Mickey Crackleton. "Your honor, we don't want to give him back," she said.

"Beg pardon."

"My husband and I have been fostering Mickey Crackleton. We ask that he remain in our care and that we be allowed to apply for adoption."

"You want to adopt my Mickey Mouse?" blurted Big Ed, seated next to Aggie. His eyes were round as goose eggs, surprised by this turn of events.

Mark the Shark swung into action. "May I point out that Mr. Edward Crackleton does not own the boy. He is merely an employer – and a great uncle perhaps."

"Where is his biological mother?" asked the Judge.

"Unknown," replied Mark Tidemore. "She abandoned the boy when he was a baby. He has been raised by various family members, passed around like a hot potato, pressed into criminal activities by Mr. Crackleton here."

"Objection," shouted Aggie, hardly believing that she was facing off against her own father.

"Sustained," responded Judge Cramer. "No evidence has been entered to substantiate that accusation."

"We are prepared to call Police Chief Harry Teague to the stand to so testify, your honor."

"No need," the judge sighed. Everybody in the county knew Big Ed was a small-town crime lord.

Aggie spoke up. "We will stipulate that everything my da— uh, Mr. Tidemore said was true, except that part about Mr. Edward Crackleton being a crook. Even if he is. I am here to represent the defendant, Mickey Crackleton. I suggest the court ask him about *his* wishes."

"Very well. Young man, do you want to remain with the Madisons and allow them to apply to adopt you?"

"You bet. I like it there. She makes a great watermelon upside down cake."

"I will take that as a yes."

"Hey," Big Ed spoke up. "What about me? Mickey Mouse was one of my best workers."

"Doing what, may I ask?" interjected Mark the Shark.

Big Ed frowned. "Uh, never mind. Your mother-in-law can have him. One less mouth for me to feed."

"Very well," said Judge Cramer. "The court remands Mickey Crackleton into the custody of Madelyn and Beauregard Madison so they can proceed with an application to adopt. Any objections, Miss Tidemore?"

"None your honor."

"Burglary charges are dismissed. Any objections, Mr. Hutchinson?"

"None."

"Mayor Tidemore?"

"None."

Judge Cramer banged down the gavel against its wooden sound block to make his decision official. "So ordered," he said. "Court dismissed."

Aggie turned to her client. "Looks like you're going to be my uncle," she said with a dazed look on her face.

"Maddy said I could have your old room."

"Take N'yen's. I may have to move back in if this lawyering thing doesn't work out."

# CHAPTER FORTY-NINE

## The Feds Show Up

"**I** need a lawyer," came Tommy Truehart's plaintive voice over the telephone.

"What did you do?" asked Aggie Tidemore.

"The FBI is accusing me of breaking into a Top-Secret database."

"Did you?"

"You know I did. But I was just looking for Fritz Berber's wife."

"Admit nothing."

"Whatever you say."

"Where are you?"

"At the police station in the interrogation room."

"Is Harry Teague there?"

"Yes, he's the one who convinced them to let me call you."

"I'll be right there. Don't go away."

"That's not likely. I'm handcuffed to a chair."

~ ~ ~

"Yes, ma'am. Mr. Truehart is facing a ten-year prison sentence for illegally obtaining National Security Information." The FBI Special Agent looked like casting out of a *Men in Black* movie, right down to the dark suit and sunglasses. His ID gave his name as Willard Blankenship. The affixed photograph was a good likeness.

"I think not," said Aggie with more courage than she'd thought she had. This was her first experience in dealing with the United States Government. Nonethless, she looked quite professional in her slimline black skirt and ruffled white blouse.

"And why not?" responded the second FBI guy. His ID gave his name as T. William Williams. His photo required a second look in that he sported a neat beard in it. His face was now smooth.

"Are you aware of the legal concept known as Ethical Hacking?

"Well, yes, but Mr. Truehart –" began the first Special Agent.

"*Deputy* Truehart," interjected Aggie. "I'm sure Chief Teague has informed you that Thomas Godfrey Truehart is one of his employees, has he not?"

"Yes, but –"

"And," she bulldogged on, "that Deputy Truehart has been investigating the murder of one Fritz Rottweiler Berber, also known as Ivor Muscovy?"

"Ma'am, that is a federal matter," said the second Special Agent patiently.

"There's been no assertion of that until now," countered Aggie. "Mr. Berber was the local mailman. His murder falls under local jurisdiction. It is only by solid, authorized police work that Chief Teague and his deputy here discovered that Fritz Berber was an undercover spy."

"Ivor Muscovy was not an undercover spy. He was a Soviet defector under witness protection," argued SA Blankenship. The small room was crowded with the two FBI men, Aggie, Chief Teague, and Tommy – as elbow-to-elbow as a Friday-night poker game.

"You knew that," Aggie asserted. "But no one from the FBI or any other government agency stepped forward to share that information when he was murdered – likely by a Russian assassin. So, the local police was merely performing its duty to investigate this suspicious death."

SA Blankenship frowned. "We understood Ivor Muscovy was shot by some little old lady. Surely, you're not suggesting she was a Russian assassin."

"No, but we believe she accidentally shot Mr. Berber while he was being attacked by a Russian assassin."

"Do you know where we can find this supposed assassin?"

"No, that's why Deputy Truehart was looking at Ivor Muscovy's records on a government database. How was he to know it was Top Secret?"

"Because it said so. Matter of fact, it took some fancy hacking to get past that firewall. Few people could do that."

Aggie felt a sense of pride, knowing it was her husband who had actually figured out how to penetrate the classified database. But she said, "Chief Teague has a very talented technical staff."

"That doesn't give Deputy Truehart the authority to access information on a highly classified database," repeated the Special Agent.

"*Au contraire*. Back to that concept of Ethical Hacking. That's an authorized attempt to gain access to a computerized database."

"His intrusion was unauthored."

"Not at all. An ethical hacker must have permission from the system owner or a law enforcement agency or a court order. Deputy Truehart represents a law enforcement agency in pursuit of its duties."

"The Computer Fraud and Abuse Act prohibits –"

"The CFAA," she interrupted, "is one of the main federal statutes used to prosecute cybercrimes. It covers a wide range of criminal activity, such as computer hacking, stealing computer data, cyber extortion, and unauthorized computer access to defraud. None of that applies here."

"Stealing federal documents is clearly illegal under CFAA," the FBI man insisted.

"But my client did not remove or retain any classified documents. Everything was untouched, merely scanned for information related to this murder investigation."

"For proper authorization, he needed a court order."

Police Chief Harry Teague spoke up. "We can clear that up for you right now," he held up a telephone. "I have Judge Horace Cramer here on the line. He will confirm that he gave us verbal consent in advance of the incursion."

"Okay, okay, never mind the judge. You obviously had good intentions. So, we're prepared to drop the matter – on one condition."

"What's that?"

"That you agree to stay out of federal databases."

# CHAPTER FIFTY

## The Library

Sissy was still making it to work, despite the morning sickness. Her mother had recommended she drink lots of ginger ale. She thought it helped a bit.

Tessie took on some extra hours, freeing the young director up for more work breaks, an afternoon nap, and leaving early. Mayor Mark Tidemore approved Tessie's overtime. "I can really use the money," she said happily. "I'm trying to save up for a new car."

"I thought Bobby Ray Purdue gave you a brand-new Mercedes," said Sissy.

"He did, but the rat had it repossessed when we broke up."

"That's the way it is with rich guys," commensurated Sissy. "They're very selfish, when you come down to it."

"Your husband N'yen is rich. Everybody knows he has a big trust fund."

"Yes, but it's never sunk in. He still saves his spare change in a piggy bank on our bedroom dresser."

~ ~ ~

"Thanks," said Tommy Truehart. "You saved my bacon with the FBI."

Aggie smiled. "That's what lawyers do. Besides, you're a member of The Quilters Club: Next Generation. We take care of our own."

"I can't believe Judge Cramer was willing to back us up with a fib about a court order."

"Caruthers Corners is kinda like a club too. We take care of our own. Besides, Horace Cramer isn't a federal judge. His loyalty to the US Government is limited. In Indiana, most trial court judges are up for election every six years. So, Judge Cramer is loyal to his constituents."

~ ~ ~

Bobby Ray Purdue looked over the report from his investigators. He would like to hire Marybell Olsen to help him manage the portfolio of gaming companies he'd been acquiring. She was obviously smart. She'd kept track of the Hoople Quadruplets household; then managed the retirement center; and now had taken over Strays & Others, that animal rescue outfit just off Burpyville Highway.

Problem was, her background check had turned up some disturbing information.

Marybelle Olsen was *not* Marybelle Olsen.

Hmph, he said to himself. Maybe he should talk with her anyway. He had an equal opportunity hiring policy. He was willing to hire imposters as well as real people.

# CHAPTER FIFTY-ONE

## Perry Mason's Paul Drake

**M**ickey Mouse was standing at Aggie's front door. She opened it with surprise. "What are you doing here?" she asked.

"Thought I'd visit my favorite niece."

"Don't get cheeky with me, you little Crackleton. I'm a dozen years older than you. Besides, your adoption has not been finalized yet."

"Will be soon enough. I like it here on the right side of the law."

"Think you can keep your nose clean? If you revert to old habits, I won't be the lawyer who bails you out."

"C'mon. I came here to do you a good turn." The boy offered a mischievous smile. She noticed he had freckles across the bridge of his nose, just like she did. Makeup usually hid hers.

"Like what?"

"When I broke into Bobby Ray Purdue's security perimeters, I thought I may as well take more than just that rusty old toolbox. While I was rummaging around in his house, I found this." He handed her a manilla envelope marked Iron Fist Enterprises.

"What's this?"

"A report from a private investigation firm that Bobby Ray uses. Thought you'd find it interesting."

"Okay." She undid the clasp and pulled out a report with a big red **CONFIDENTIAL** stamp at the top of the page. She skimmed the first page. "Hmm," she said, "this *is* interesting."

"Told you it was."

"Mickey, you and I might become good friends after all. How would you like to be my official investigator. Every law office needs one."

"You mean like Paul Drake in all them *Perry Mason* reruns on TV?"

"Exactly like that. You do good work," she tapped the confidential report with her forefinger. "This might just crack a case for me."

"You sure you want to hire me? I'm only twelve, you know."

"No problem. I'll pay you off the books."

"How much?'

"Enough to keep you happy."

"Does that mean I can have your old bedroom?"

"Don't get overeager," she winked. "But we can talk about that later."

# CHAPTER FIFTY-TWO

## A Generous Offer

**B**obby Ray Purdue sent word that he'd like to meet with N'yen. Having a Hoople trust fund, N'yen was comfortably wealthy; but Bobby Ray was many times richer, the result of a pile of rare Grand Watermelon dollars found stuffed inside his grandmother's quilt. When a multimillionaire summoned you, you came.

N'yen wore his best suit for the meeting. Bobby Ray was dressed in Hugh Hefner pajamas, oblivious of his unruly hair and unshaven cheeks. "Been a busy week," he said by way of explanation.

"You wanted to see me?"

"Darn tootin' I did. Everybody says you're the smartest guy in town. I want you to work for me."

"Doing what?" N'yen adjusted the round Harry Potter spectacles on his nose.

"Whatever you want. You're brilliant, you'll figure out something."

"That's a very generous offer, sir. But I prefer to continue my astrophysics work."

"That's it then," Bobby Ray snapped his fingers. "We'll build you an observatory out in the field behind my house. Cookie Bentley has agreed to sell me the land. You can be like a SETI facility, searching for aliens, looking for UFOs."

"They call them UAPs now."

"What the heck, flying saucers. I'd like to own one of them."

"Good luck with that."

~ ~ ~

Bobby Ray named a high figure, by N'yen had all the money he needed, and besides he liked writing for *Scientific American*. "No thanks," he said.

"What if I doubled it?"

"I'm happy as thing are," N'yen said apologetically.

"Oh well, I gave it the old college try," said Bobby Ray – although he'd never gone to college, having spent those years with a circus. But he was a helluva juggler and could walk a tightrope.

"Before I go, can I ask you an impertinent question?"

Bobby Ray looked up. "Those are the best kind."

"Why did you really shoot your brother. I don't believe it was over a tricycle."

"You are a smart guy," allowed Bobby Ray. "I'm impressed enough to tell you the truth – but it's gotta be our secret. No tattling to Chief Teague, agreed?"

"Agreed."

"I shot him because if he were dead, I'd inherit everything. I've seen his will. I'm his sole heir."

"You're as rich as he is. Why would you need more?"

"Richer," he bragged. "And it's not about need ... it's about more. Having a lot of money is fun. Having more money is more fun. Some people collect video games. I collect gaming companies."

N'yen hesitated, but said it anyway. "You know, when you talk like that, you sound a trifle mad."

"Maybe I am," he chuckled. "I want to add my brother's fortune to my own. Then I'd be really wealthy. Guess I'll just have to find a better way to kill him."

"You may be too late. I hear he changed his will this week. Cut you out. Left it all to a ..."

"Well, I'll be a monkey's backside. I shoulda known he'd do something like that. He was always trying to screw up my plans. That's why I left home in the first place, disappearing with those other three boys into Neverending Swamp. I shoulda just stayed gone."

"Then you'd never have had all your toys – the dino skeleton, that WW2 biplane, all those gaming companies."

"True," he admitted. "But I still wish I'd hit my brother in a more vital spot. It might be years before he dies of natural causes."

~ ~ ~

"Why doesn't anyone want to work for me?" Bobby Ray lamented as he walked N'yen to his car. "I want to build new businesses like Elon Musk or Richard Branson. But everybody I try to hire turns me down."

"Who else has turned you down?"

"That haughty British woman who used to manage the Hoople household."

"Mrs. Olsen?"

"That's the one. I wanted her to help me manage my growing business empire – I'm buying a lot of gaming companies – but she turned me down to run a dog park."

"An animal rescue shelter," N'yen corrected him. "I think you helped fund it."

"Oh, right."

"Goodbye, sir. You have a nice day."

"Wait, I have another idea. You're working for that magazine *Scientific American*. What if I buy it and let you run it for me?"

"I don't think it's for sale."

"Everything is for sale, my friend."

"How did you know I'm working for *Scientific American*? Do you read my articles?"

"No, no. I prefer comic books and graphic novels. I have everyone I try to hire investigated. Can't be too careful these days."

"You had me investigated?"

"Extensively. For instance, I know that you've discovered two quasars. That you got airsick the first time you flew on a plane. And that you have a mole on your left shoulder ... don't worry, it isn't cancerous."

"You do that with everyone you try to hire?"

"Of course. I even know you just finished writing an article on the Voyager spacecrafts. And that your wife is pregnant."

"How do you know that? We haven't even told my parents yet."

"Oh, I know lots of things. For example, Tessie Humphrey is embezzling money from the library fund. Old Tom Dancy, the county clerk, is sleeping with his secretary. And MaryBelle Olsen isn't really British."

"What?"

"That's right. She's actually a Russian. I think she's just putting on airs with that phony British accent."

# CHAPTER FIFTY-THREE

## Spilling All the Dirt

"How was your day?" N'yen asked his wife when she got home from the library.

"Morning sickness wasn't too bad today. I think all that ginger ale is helping. How was your day, Sweetie Pie?"

"Turned down a job offer from Bobby Ray Purdue," said N'yen. He felt boastful over his refusal to be bought.

"Doing what?"

"I don't know. He's just on an OCD mission to hire some folks so he can feel like a captain of industry."

Sissy giggled at that. "Does he actually own any industries?"

"Says he's buying up gaming companies."

She rolled her eyes. "Just a way to get free games, I'd bet."

"Probably." He helped Sissy ease into a comfortable chair and remove her tight shoes. Her feet were starting to swell a bit. Pregnancy was a constant discomfort so far.

"By the way," he said, "Tessie is embezzling from the library fund."

"How would you know that?"

"Bobby Ray told me. He also said Tom Dancy's having an affair with Mitzi Templeton."

"Wasn't she Aggie's dad's old secretary?"

"I think they call them administrative assistants nowadays."

"You know what I mean."

"As I recall, Mitzi had a big crush on Mark the Shark. That's why he transferred her over to Old Tom."

"Well, if what you say is true, she must have a thing for bosses. Some women are drawn to authority figures."

"Is that your attraction to me?"

"No, Dearest Heart. I simply think you have a cute bum."

"Cecilia LaToya Jackson Madison, you're a very naughty girl."

"Course I am. How do you think I got pregnant?"

"Oh, one other thing."

"What's that?"

"I found out who's the other Soviet defector."

# CHAPTER FIFTY-FOUR

## The Young Quiltmakers

Sissy called a meeting of The Quilter Club: Next Generation. The four of them – Aggie, N'yen, Sissy, and Tommy – met at the sewing room in the Hoople Quilting Heritage Museum, just like their namesakes used to do. Aunt Lizzie had figured out what was going on, but kept quiet about it. She would tell Maddy and her friends when the time came.

"What's up?" said Aggie.

"N'yen and I know who the other defector is," Sissy announced with a sense of triumph.

"That's right," smiled N'yen, always happy to be one up on his cousin.

"Marybelle Olsen," shrugged Aggie.

"*Eiik*! How did you know?" Sissy demanded. Her surprise foiled.

"Yes, how?" echoed N'yen.

"My investigator turned up a confidential report in Bobby Ray's file cabinet."

"You broke into Bobby Ray's again?" said Tommy.

"No, my investigator found it the first time."

"What investigator?" frowned N'yen. "The first time – digging up that old toolbox – was that Crackleton kid, Mickey Mouseketeer."

"Mickey Mouse," Aggie corrected. "Better get his name right. He's soon going to be your uncle."

"Oh, that adoption thing. I hadn't considered that."

"Grammy and Grampy will want us to accept him into the family ... just like everyone did with you, N'yen."

"Okay, I get it."

Aggie winked. "The kid's a slick thief. We want him on our side. I propose we invite him to join The Quilters Club: Next Generation as a junior member, just like we used to be."

"Alright," nodded Sissy.

"Sure, why not?" agreed N'yen.

"Here, here," added Tommy. After all, charges against the boy had been dropped. And, without Aggie's intervention, he might have become a felon himself.

"One more thing," said Aggie.

"What's that?"

"I think the name The Quilters Club: Next Generation is dorky. I suggest we change it to The Young Quiltmakers. Simpler, more straightforward."

"Why does it have to be about quilting?" complained Tommy Truehart. He thought quilting was "sissy."

Aggie patted him on the hand. "It's our cover. We can't go around calling ourselves The Young Detectives. Everybody would know what we're up to."

"Yes, pretending to be quilters gives us an edge," agreed N'yen. He had long ago made his peace with quiltmaking. Over the years, he had completed two patchwork quilts himself.

"What do you mean, pretending?" snapped his wife. "Aggie and I are pretty darn good quilters. Aunt Lizzie taught us herself."

"Okay, okay. Don't go getting your panties in a bunch."

"You'll leave my panties out of this if you ever expect to have a second child."

"Hey, I'd like to have a big family. The more the merrier. Maybe a dozen."

"Don't get overambitious, Buster. You're already on thin ice with me. Even a second child is iffy."

Must be those hormones kicking up, thought Aggie. So she changed the subject, coming to her cousin's rescue. "About Marybelle Olsen –" she said.

"Yeah," nodded Tommy, happy to shift topics. A single guy, he didn't even have a girlfriend – unless you counted the Andrew Sisters. Not that those wayward twins could be counted as being anyone's girlfriends. Dating them wasn't as much a commitment as a habit.

N'yen appreciated the intervention. "So what do we do about Anna Petrova Muscovy?" he asked.

# CHAPTER FIFTY-FIVE

## Completing the Assignment

**M**arybelle Olsen was locking up at Strays & Others for the day. She was running a little late because she had to give a pill to a Rottweiler, no easy task if you want to keep your fingers ... or arm. But Feisty had been a doll despite her name, taking the medication with one wet slurp.

Marybelle didn't see the burly man getting out of a pickup truck on the far side of the parking lot. Mikhail Slovak (his real name was Leonid Berezovsky) had stolen the Ford F-150 earlier in the day from the Food Lion parking lot. He had been patiently waiting here for the woman to leave work. No more poisons, he would simply garrote her and be done with it. He would return to Mother Russia by way of Canada to Helsinki, then to Moscow.

In a very few minutes, his assignment would be completed – both Ivor Muscovy and his wife Anna dispatched.

~ ~ ~

Asking if they could use the Quilting Heritage Museum's computer, the newly anointed Young Quiltmakers surround the cluttered desk in Lizzie's office. "You're sure she's at Strays & Others?" asked Tommy Truehart.

"She should be leaving soon," said Aggie. Having just adopted her dog from there, she knew the hours.

"Okay, here goes. The deputy typed in a few passwords to get started. As one of his side jobs, he had installed the security system at Strays & Others, a series of door and window alarms as well as several surveillance cameras. He could access them from this desktop.

*Click, click, click.*

There she was, Marybelle Olsen locking up for the day. But wait – there on camera 2, the one overlooking the parking lot, was a large man climbing out of a pickup truck. It looked like the Ford F-150 that Fatty Johnson had reported stolen just this afternoon. The guy looked threatening.

Tommy and his friends were ten minutes away, which might be too late ... but wasn't Deputy Rufus Barnswell patrolling somewhere in that vicinity? Or how about Carlton Yosterman, the high school resource officer? The school was near the animal shelter.

"Hurry up, do something," urged Aggie, gaping at the screen.

"Gimme a sec," muttered Tommy as he picked up the telephone and dialed the police station. "Myrtle," he shouted, "put out a call for anyone out there to proceed to Strays & Others. Highest alert – crime in progress!"

"I'm Elvira," the dispatcher said as she picked up her microphone.

~ ~ ~

As it happened, Gus Bentley was on his way to Wabash Acres to apply for a night security job. He was just approaching the turnoff for Strays & Others when he heard the call. As a policeman, he'd had a radio in his car. He'd forgotten to turn it in when he quit.

"... crime in progress."

Without thinking, he gave the steering wheel a hard right turn, swinging into the animal shelter's parking lot. Straight ahead, he saw Marybelle Olsen struggling with a large man with closely cropped gray hair. She pushed the man away and started to run. The assailant started after her, but Gus accelerated, his car clipping the man with a loud *thump*! The impact broke the right headlight and tossed the man into the air. He landed with a second *thump*! on the rough gravel of the parking lot. There was a fair amount of blood.

Screeching to a stop, Gus fumbling in his glove box until he found the pair of handcuffs he'd abandoned there, then leapt out of the car and clicked them onto the assailant's wrists.

Climbing to his feet, Gus could feel his legs trembling. His heart was pounding from all the adrenaline. He turned to Marybelle Olsen and forced himself to speak: "Are you all right, ma'am?"

"Gus," she said carefully. "Call Chief Teague. I have something to confess."

# EPILOGUE

## The Next Generation

**A**ggie was successful in getting a Not Guilty verdict for Birdie Longstreet, citing the Castle Doctrine.

The term comes from English common-law wherein every person's home is considered his or her "Castle." Indiana is one of some thirty-one states that have adopted the concept of "standing one's ground" as a part of the affirmative defense for protecting an individual's home and curtilage. This provides for the use of deadly force without retreating.

The jury agreed that the elderly lady had every reason to fear for her life when a man was trying to break down her door, no matter how legitimate his reason.

Miss Birdie thought her appearance in court was an episode of *Judge Judy*. She enjoyed it thoroughly.

The Feds took away Leonid Berezovsky. Nobody ever heard what happened to him; he simply "disappeared into the system." Some said the CIA was involved.

Marybelle Olsen (Anna Petrova Muscovy, that is) was relocated as part of the Witness Protection Program. Her and her husband's defection had provided useful information to the US government; the reward was her continued safety.

Nobody knew where Marybelle was sent. That's the whole point of assuming a new identity. However, Maddy Madison once received a postcard from St. Petersburg, Florida, with the cryptic message:

It's warmer here than my St. Petersburg.

Gus Bentley was offered his old job back, but he turned it down. Chief Harry Teague was disappointed. However, Gus was pleased with his new career choice: He replaced Fritz Berber as the town's mailman. As a once-shunned Crackleton, he liked being now accepted by his neighbors.

Sissy Madison had a baby girl. N'yen was a nervous but proud father. He also discovered a third quasar. He named it after his daughter Marybelle.

Mickey Mouse was fitting into the Madison household just fine. He had taken Aggie's old room after all (it was bigger than N'yen's). Beau was teaching him to fish. But, to date, nobody had caught The Monster – jig and pig or not.

After a zillion terms, Mark Tidemore retired as Mayor of Caruthers Corners, turning over the reins to his daughter Agnes. Like her father, she won by a landslide. As it happened, Aggie was the youngest mayor in the town's 200-year history. The job seemed fitting, in that she was a direct descendent of Col. Beauregard Hollingsworth Madison, one of the three Town Founders.

As for those young amateur sleuths, one case was enough. But the coterie of off-the-books detectives – Aggie, N'yen, Sissy, and Tommy – remain ready to swing back into action if any crime needed solving in Caruthers Corners.

It could happen.

✳ ✳ ✳

Thank you for reading.
Please review this book. Reviews
help others find Absolutely Amazing eBooks and
inspire us to keep providing these marvelous tales.
If you would like to be put on our email list
to receive updates on new releases,
contests, and promotions, please go to
AbsolutelyAmazingEbooks.com and sign up.

# ABOUT THE AUTHOR

**Marjory Sorrell Rockwell** says needlecraft arts – quilting, crocheting, knitting – are pastimes every woman can appreciate. And she particularly loves quiltmaking. "It's like painting with cloth," she says. But when not quilting she writes mysteries about a Midwestern sleuth not unlike herself, a middle-aged lady with an unpredictable family and loyal friends. And she's a big fan of watermelon pie.

Quilter Club Mysteries

# Visit Maddy's new website...

### quiltersclubmysteries.com/

Take a tour of Caruthers Corners and the surrounding countryside. Meet Maddy's family and friends. Get a complete list of all the characters who have appeared in the entire Quilters Club Mysteries book series. Well, practically all.

What's more, you'll learn lots about quilting. There's a free quilt pattern. A dictionary of quilting terms. Even a Quilt Gallery showing some of Maddy's favorite quilt patterns.

No fees, no charges. Just fun.

For sales, editorial information, subsidiary rights information
or a catalog, please write or phone or e-mail
AbsolutelyAmazingBooks
Manhanset House
Shelter Island Hts., New York 11965-0342, US
Tel: 212-427-7139
www.AbsolutelyAmazingEbooks.com
bricktower@aol.com
www.IngramContent.com

www.ingramcontent.com/pod-product-compliance
Lightning Source LLC
Chambersburg PA
CBHW071835020726
47502CB00004B/1375